BORN HEARTLESS III

T.J. Edwards

Lock Down Publications and Ca$h
Presents
BORN HEARTLESS III
A Novel by *T.J. Edwards*

Born Heartless 3

Lock Down Publications
P.O. Box 870494
Mesquite, Tx 75187

Lock Down Publications
Like our page on Facebook: Lock Down
Publications @
www.facebook.com/lockdownpublications.ldp
Cover design and layout by: **Dynasty Cover Me**
Book interior design by: **Shawn Walker**
Edited by**: Sunny Giovanni**

Stay Connected with Us!

Text **LOCKDOWN** to 22828 to stay up-to-date with new releases, sneak peaks, contests and more…

Thank you!

Submission Guideline.

Submit the first three chapters of your completed manuscript to ldpsubmissions@gmail.com, subject line: Your book's title. The manuscript must be in a .doc file and sent as an attachment. Document should be in Times New Roman, double spaced and in size 12 font. Also, provide your synopsis and full contact information. If sending multiple submissions, they must each be in a separate email.

Have a story but no way to send it electronically? You can still submit to LDP/Ca$h Presents. Send in the first three chapters, written or typed, of your completed manuscript to:

LDP: Submissions Dept
P.O. Box 870494
Mesquite, Tx 75187

DO NOT send original manuscript. Must be a duplicate.

Provide your synopsis and a cover letter containing your full contact information.

Thanks for considering LDP and Ca$h Presents.

T.J. Edwards

Chapter 1

I pushed the Chanel sunglasses up on my nose to block out the brightness of the Jamaican sun as I stepped off of the plane. There was a slight breeze. It smelled like ocean water. My clothes waved like a flag as I pulled my suitcase out of the airport, and to the curb.

Juelz lowered his Tom Ford sunglasses and peeped two thick ass Jamaican females as they walked past us with their asses shaking like a ma'fucka. Both were high yellow with long ass braids. He shook his head. "Nigga, I swear to God we hitting up the beach. I gotta see what all ass this ma'fucka got to offer." He said, still peeping the girls.

I laughed. "Shorty n'em thick as a muthafucka." I had to admit. I said it loud enough for them to hear me. They stopped and looked like they wanted to come back to see what was good. I threw my arms up. The sunlight shined off of my two chains. The diamonds in my TJ piece sparkled like a kaleidoscope.

Before they could make it back to us, Jackie blocked their path, and got wagging her finger. "Unn. Unn, lil' girls. Y'all gon' 'bout ya' business. These boys already spoken for." She told them.

"What?" Juelz stepped around her. "Yo, she tripping. What's good? Me and my brother tryna see what it do?" He jacked. His gold chains were shining just as hard. He had a piece that was of the Puerto Rican flag. It glistened in the light.

"Juelz, stop playing with me. Y'all ain't down here for them lil' hoes. Ya' hear for me. Now let's go." She chastised him.

I was already Facebooking Sodi. I was telling her how much I loved and missed her. She had already told me that while I was away that it was all she wanted to hear from me until I got back. She had plans on spending some time with her mother and siblings which I thought was cool. I honestly did miss her. At the same time, I couldn't get Punkin out of my brain either.

Jackie snatched my cellphone out of my hand all rude and shit. "Gimme this."

"Bitch." I grabbed my shit back. "Don't be snatching shit out of my hand. You got me fucked up." I took a step toward her.

She backed up. "Calm down, TJ. All I'm asking is that y'all give me my due while we're here. If y'all wanna be on your phones, and fuck off with some of the locals, that's fine, but just don't let me see it. I'm paying all of this money because I wanna have a good time with the both of y'all, and I want it to be special for me. Got it?"

"Yeah, I do, but if you snatch anything out of my hands again, you gon' be floating in that ma'fuckin' ocean. That's my word." I meant that shit too.

Juelz laughed, and slid his arm around her neck. "Baby, it's good. We finna treat this body right. You got us. Don't even trip, but you ain't gotta be all overbearing either. That ain't cool." He kissed her cheek.

8

She looked up at him. "Well, there are a bunch of beautiful young women down here. I can't help but to feel insecure. Y'all gon' have to help me with that along the way." She said this last part looking directly at me. "What's the matter with you, TJ?"

"Nothing. Come on. Let's get this show on the road." I said, stepping up to the Navigator limousine as it pulled up to the curb.

Two Jamaican handlers got out to assist us with our bags. I saw that Jackie went all out for this trip. I guessed a certain part of me felt that it was only right that me and Juelz gave her exactly what she was paying for.

Juelz helped her inside of the truck. Then once all of us were in and situated, he popped a bottle of Moët, and poured her a glass. "Here you go, ma. I want you to have the first glass because you are the most special person here right now." He winked at me.

"Awww-uh, thank you, baby. I needed to hear that." She kissed his lips and snuggled against him. After a few seconds she patted the seat next to her. "Come here, TJ."

I turned off my phone and got up, sitting beside her. Once there I went into mission mode. I rested my hand on her right thick thigh and caressed it. "You been missing yo' baby?"

She bit into her bottom lip. "Yeah. A whole, whole lot."

I slid my hand under her shirt. Her chocolate thighs were real thick, and healthy. I had to admit for an older woman Jackie kept her body right. While I rubbed her thigh, I took the time to squeeze it just to feel the firmness of each one. She moaned and opened her thighs wider. Now I was rubbing over her the front of her panties. The lips felt meaty.

Juelz slid his hand into her top. He pulled out her right breast, and flicked his tongue over her nipple, before he sucked on it has if he was trying to get some milk out of her. "You like that, baby, huh?"

"Yes. Mmm-hmm." She opened her thighs even wider.

I slid two fingers into her box, and casually ran them in and out. She was wet. Dripping her juices. My thumb would stop and rotate circles all over her clitoris that was standing up like a pinky finger.

"Go down on me, TJ. Please, baby. I need you to taste this pussy. I miss the way you do it." She moaned, as Juelz pulled out both of her breasts, and squeezed them together.

I slid to the carpeted limousine floor onto knees. Cocked her thighs wide open for old time sake and planted soft kisses on each thigh. She moaned and arched her back. My soft kisses turned into bites. Every time I rose from one place, I saw that I left a wet mark behind, then I was assaulting the next spot. My fingers dipped into her pussy deeper and deeper.

"Eat me, baby. Please. Unn. I can take this shit. I need to feel your mouth on my pussy. Y'all my boys." She placed her right foot up on the seat, busting her cat wide open. Her sex lips were dark chocolate. Her insides were bubblegum pink like a rare steak once you cut into it.

I blew on her pearl and kissed it. She shivered. My tongue lashed out and flicked it ten quick times. Then I slurped it into my mouth as if it were an oyster.

Jackie placed her thighs on my shoulders and pulled me to her in a death clutch. She rode my face hard, until she came, screaming at the top of her lings how much she missed me. I couldn't breathe. I just kept my tongue out and dug my nails into her legs. When she finally opened them, I was still licking and sucking like I was hungry. She had been the first woman to have taught me how to eat pussy, and now here she was reaping the benefits. Her pussy juice slid down my chin, and onto my neck.

Juelz pulled out his piece and grabbed a handful of her hair. "Come on, bitch. You already know what yo' baby want."

She licked her lips and sucked him into her mouth. The next thing I knew, she was sucking him fast-paced, slurping, and making a whole bunch of noise.

I leaned her on her side and raised her thigh into my right forearm. My rubber was already in place. With one forward motion of my hips, I slid into her, and yanked that ass back to me by use of her hips. Found my rhythm and got to fucking her for all she was worth; dipping into her tight box. She used her inner muscles on me almost immediately. Showing me what that vet shit was all about.

Juelz's eyes rolled into the back of his head. He jumped into her mouth again and again. "Her head game. Uh. Uh. Shit. This bitch." He kept humping. His eyelids closed tighter.

Jackie kept bobbing. She pulled her mouth from his piece and screamed as she felt me cumming hard. Her pussy muscles had worked me over. She pumped Juelz's pipe until he started to bust. It spit up onto her face, before she sucked him back into her mouth hungrily. He jerked and tried to push her off of him, but she had him in a death clutch it seemed.

I pulled out and took the rubber off. My dick kept jumping. The sight of her chocolate titties with the Hershey Kiss nipples were hot to me. I stroked my pipe for a few moments, looking at her chest.

After twenty minutes of us getting warmed up, the limousine pulled into the Paradise Island Resort that we were to be staying at. The handlers got out of the limo and knocked on the back doors. We were all just getting dressed. I was sure they smelled a wave of sex as soon as the doors were opened.

I climbed out and headed inside. Turned my phone back on and called Sodi. It may sound crazy, but I just wanted to hear her voice. I was missing her for some reason. Her phone kept ringing and ringing, and then it went straight to voicemail. That worried me, but I tried my best to not panic.

***

As soon as we got into the presidential suite, Jackie stopped in the middle of the floor, and dropped her clothes. "What do you say you come and take a shower with me, TJ, while Juelz roll us up a couple blunts?" She walked up to me and stopped in my face.

"That sound like a plan. Come on."

She took off walking in front of me. Her ass jiggling the whole way. She was a bad older bitch. Fine and chocolate. All it took was for me to tune into her body parts and I found myself lost all over again. That was that vet magic. I felt like only a sexy ass older woman could place that kind of spell over me.

She turned on the shower, and got the temperatures set just right while I got undressed and rubbed all over that big ass of hers. By the time we stepped inside, I was rock hard. I pushed her up against the wall. She placed her foot on the rim of the tub. I slid the Magnum down and dove into that pussy with a vengeance. Damn near picking her up with each thrust. I got to digging deep. She moaned with her face in the crux of my neck.

"Mmm. Mmm. Mmm. Fuck me, baby. Fuck me. Yes. Aww, shit I missed you. Awww. Awww. Shit."

I grabbed her thigh tighter and kept piping with my knees bent. "Shit, ma. Shit. This vet pussy. This that vet pussy."

She jumped and wrapped both of her thighs around me. I had to catch my balance, and crash into the tiled wall with her. Once there, I bounced her, giving her all of me. "Yes! Yes. Awww! Baby! This dick! Ooo, shit!" She licked along my neck and sucked on the thick vein there. I felt that pussy shaking as she came, screaming at the top of her lungs.

I busted again and pulled out. "Bitch, bend yo' ass over this ma'fuckin' tub. Hurry up!"

She made the transition on wobbly legs. She bent over and looked back at me. That chocolate ass was round. There were a few stretch marks across it that made it look super sexy too. Her pussy looked like it was breathing. The lips were slightly open. I rubbed into them and pinched her clit. She shrieked. "Fuck me, baby. I need you. Fuck me as hard as you can. Punish me."

I leaned down and kissed her right on both cheeks. They were hot. Then I got to rubbing all over them before my hand rose high. I brought it back down fast and hard. *Smack!*

She nearly stood up. "Uhhhh! Baby!"

Smack! I rubbed all over that ass again, and then dipped down and played with that leaking pussy. It dribbled all down her inner thighs. "You like that, ma? Huh?"

She looked over her shoulder at me with her eyes full of lust. Her tongue traced a circle around her lips. "It's time, lil' daddy. Fuck me, baby. Make me scream out. Please."

I grabbed her hips aggressively, and slammed home. My nails dug into her flesh while I pounded her strapped ass as hard as I could, watching my shit go in and out of her.

"Oh. Oh. Oh. Shit. Lil' daddy. My baby. Awww. Noooo. Shit, it hurt. Mmm. Baby. Baby." She arched her back again, and thaw her head back, screaming at the top of her lungs. Then she was cumming all over me.

Juelz stepped into the bathroom, smoking on a blunt. "Damn. Shorty, it sound like you in this ma'fucka killing her ass." He blew his smoke to the ceiling. "Switch, my nigga. You take the weed, and I'ma take mama."

She shivered at hearing him refer her as that. My dick slipped out of her, and rested against her ass, still rock hard. I circled her asshole with my middle finger. "Juelz, you ever hit this ass back here? Seeing as you done did everything else to my vet bitch?"

He shook his head. "N'all, not yet. But shorty 'bout ready to give her baby some of that back doe, ain't you, mama?"

I grabbed her by the hair and yanked her head backward. "Bitch, I wish you would say yeah. You already know who this shit belong to. Don't you?"

"Yes, baby." She looked so vulnerable.

I bent down and opened them chocolate ass cheeks. Her rosebud winked at me. Before I could even think about it, my lips were covering her asshole, and my tongue was shooting in and out of her. I was slobbering on purpose. Once I got it nice and wet, I got to easing into her. Pulling back on her hair.

She shuddered with every inch that I drove into her. "Lil' daddy. Ooo. You so big. It's too big."

I rubbed her pussy juices around the entrance before I slammed home. She hollered again. I didn't give a fuck. That back doe was super tight, and hot. It got me to shaking while I smacked those cheeks and fucked her like it was new pussy.

She bounced back into me. She kept looking over her shoulders at me. "You're fucking my ass, baby. Uhhhh, shit. You're fucking me back there. Ooo. Ooo. His dick in me."

I was plunging faster and faster. Her ass got to making all kinds of noise. Her pussy leaked wetly. I slammed into her fifty hard times, and then pulled out and pulled my rubber off, cumming all over her big ass. I opened the cheeks and sprayed her asshole and everything. She reached under her stomach and played with her clit while she moaned louder and louder, cumming all over her fingers.

Juelz stood there shaking his head. "I see we on some competing shit with Jackie ass. Aiight, fool. Bet those. I'ma let that bitch get cleaned up, then it's my turn to break her ass off."

I laughed and rubbed my piece all over her lips until she opened up. When she got to sucking, my toes curled. Juelz left the room defeated. I didn't give no fuck. Wasn't no nigga 'bout to fuck in my business when it came to hitting no pussy. I didn't give a fuck if he was my nigga or not.

Chapter 2

"Yo, that bitch got some good ass pussy to be as old as she is, don't she?" Juelz asked, passing me some of that Jamaican bomb that he rolled up.

I sat back in the passenger's seat high as a kite. We had been fucking Jackie for damn near ten hours straight. It was the next day, at eleven in the morning, and I was still tired as a muthafucka. "She straight, bruh, but it's only so many positions she can be fucked in before that shit start to get repetitive. I'm missing Chicago like a ma'fucka. What's good with this Blue nigga?"

Juelz smiled. "You already know that's what we on. Jay gave me one of his connects' information down here in Kingston. We finna roll through this bitch and get us a few weapons, then we gon' catch Blue at this lil' gathering tonight down by the ocean. Shannon out here with him. I don't know how she convinced him to let her come, but she here. She clocking him every step of the way for me. She done screenshotted him a few times."

"That's what's up." I looked to my right and saw that we were rolling down a long road that was on the side of the beach. From my vantage point, the water looked like crystal blue mouthwash. I had never seen water look so pretty. Outside of it was white sand, and a sea of bad bitches. I caught sight of one right after the next.

"You seem like something ain't right. What's up?"

"Huh? Aw, nothing. I was just looking out at them hoes. I ain't seen one skinny one yet. Fuck they feeding them out here?"

"I don't know, but when it's all said and done, this is where I'm trying to move to. I can never get enough of looking at and taking down a thick bitch. It just ain't nothing like it. My bitches gotta have at least a thirty-eight around the ass. Anything else is baby food." Juelz said, laughing. "You figure out when you gone tell Sodi about Punkin being pregnant?"

I shook my head. "Hell n'all. I ain't trying to wreck her like that. She already been through enough. Sooner or later I know I gotta tell her, but right now I gotta get some other shit in order first."

Juelz nodded. "That's understandable. I think shorty love you too much to leave. I mean, I know she gon' get on yo' ass, I just don't know to what extent." He peered out at the beach and beeped his horn at a group of red bones that were walking along the sand in just a G-string. Their yellow asses bounced with each step that they took.

"Nigga, how could you ever be put into a position like the one you're in when there are so many bitches in this world? Did you just see how thick them hoes were that I beeped the horn at?"

"I did. So what?"

"So how the fuck could you be worried about whether you and Sodi are going to make it when you can replace her with the next bad bitch?" He took the blunt from me and started to puff on it.

18

"Bruh, just 'cause a bitch look bad don't mean that she gon' be about something. This girl held down eight months with no effort. She made sure I had money on my books, and she never missed a visit unless we discussed that it ahead of time. That's a good girl."

"Yeah, but how do you know that it's a million other bitches that wouldn't have done the same thing?"

"I don't."

"My point exactly. You don't know because you are only casting your net out so far. It's plenty loyal, bad bitches in the world. You only got one when you could have so many more. That shit seem stupid to me."

I mugged his goofy ass. "So, you telling me that you ain't never been in love with a female before?"

"Never have, and I never will. Unless they come out with a new bill that's more than a hundred with a bitch's face on it. Other that, I'm good. If you don't love, then you can't be hurt. My heart blacker than Whoopi Goldberg's gums, nigga, and it's gon' stay that way." He took four hard pulls and tried to hand me back the Ganja. It was almost the size of a roach.

I declined. I didn't like my fingers getting all black and shit from it. "Well, my reality is that I love Sodi. I love her to death, and sooner or later, I'ma make her my wife. The only fucked up thing about that is that I got this shorty on the way by Punkin."

"How do you feel about her?"

"I got love for her too."

"That's yo' problem, nigga. Yo' household was so fucked up that now you're trying to dish that love out to these hoes that you never got a chance to get from yo' own people. That shit sound cool, but in the end that's gon' be the death of yo' ass. Bitches love too hard. Very rarely are they willing to take a loss after they grow nuts about you. Especially if they feel like you love them too. That's why I let they ass know out the gate that I ain't going. I'm addicted to money and pussy. Those are the two things that I love. And you of course. Other than those three, fuck 'em. That's how I feel, and you should too. After all, you already know that we were both born heartless."

I sat there in my seat a bit lost. I wondered how Juelz could be like he was. That nigga fucked with plenty hoes and had a bunch of kids. I couldn't believe that he didn't love any of the ones that had pushed his seeds out, or any other one for that matter. That was so hard to believe. But I had to. What reason did he have to lie to me? All I knew was that I loved Sodi, and I wanted to do right by her. I also couldn't leave Punkin to fend for herself with a child. Only bitch niggas allowed for a woman to raise their seed on their own, and there was no bitch or hoe in me. I had to figure shit out real quick.

***

Juelz slammed the trunk to the Benz that we were rolling around Kingston in, and slid back into the driver's seat. It was nine o'clock at night and we were inside of a rundown part of the island. It looked like a third world country and smelled even worst. The people used all kinds of scrap metal to build their shacks. Everywhere I looked there was a clothesline with a bunch of clothes hanging out to dry. There were streetlights, but out of the eight present, six of them were blinking on and off as if they were threatening to go out. More than a few big ass mosquitoes landed on the windshield, along with a bunch of other bugs. I knew that they carried something that would get me sick as a muthafucka.

"Yo', we good to go. I got enough firepower in the trunk to light up Jamaica like a muthafucka. Here. Carry this for now." He handed me a .38 Special that looked like it was tarnished.

"Bruh, what the fuck I'm 'pose to do with this old ass gun? This ma'fucka look like they just pulled it out of the ocean."

"That bitch got six shots; you better use it. Them the only hand pistols they had right now. I got two Choppahs in the trunk though, and a bunch of clips. Stop being so fucking bougee, nigga. This ain't Chicago where you can just look on the ground and find a fully automatic. Besides, the only other one I got is this Desert Eagle. It got a silencer on it. We gon' need it for this move we about to put down. You gon' have to make do."

I kept the gun on my lap after checking the chamber. "Yo, it's good. Let's go fuck up homeboy."

Juelz smiled. "After we do him in though, we gotta get up with some of the locals. Ain't no way I'm coming all the way down to Jamaica and not fuck one of the bitches from this region. That would be a travesty." He started the engine and rolled off.

"So, what we finna do?"

"They having this lil' beach party on the eastside of the island tonight. Blue invested his money into a few of the local rappers out of Chicago. They are having an album release party. A release party that we about to crash and handle this business. The goal is to get that nigga to come to the bathroom. Once there, I'ma slice his throat. Then we gotta hit his artist too. That was the other move that Jay was talking about."

"So, which one you want me to hit?" I asked, seeing a group of Jamaicans mugging the car as we rolled by. They looked dirty. Their eyes were bloodshot red.

"Since that nigga Blue supposed to have a contract with Deion for you, it seems that it's only right that you change his ass." Whenever somebody in Chicago said the word *change* on some street shit, that meant to kill a person.

"Bet those. But it's finna be plenty of people here. How we gon' pull this off?"

"I got this. You just be ready to handle yo' business."

***

The ocean seemed like a desolate and scary place as we walked along the sand beside it toward the crowd of people that were gathered for Tank's album release party. I didn't know who the lil' nigga was and had never heard of him. But apparently, he was killing it on the underground scene in Chicago, and the Cartel thought he was fit to go mainstream. They fronted Blue a lot of dope so he could build up the capital to push and promote Tank, and now that he had him where he was supposed to be, Blue apparently had not been able to pay back his loan, and in the Cartel world, that meant death.

Juelz came closer to me and whispered, "If you look to your right over there, you gon' see a spot where the bathrooms are. You should go into the men's and wait for Blue to burn his bitch ass in there. I need to set it up so that he come your way."

I looked to my right just past the sound stage. I saw a little area that had a bunch of bathroom doors on them. To the left of them were a bunch of equipment that I guessed the musicians were getting ready to move onto the stage. "Aiight, that sound like a plan, but where you finna be?"

He nodded over, and I saw his baby mother coming into our direction. Her long hair flowed behind her. She had on an evening gown, barefooted. "Yo', I'm finna walk off so she can meet me under the darkness over there." He pointed with his head toward a place right by the water where there were no lights. "Be in the bathroom in thirty minutes. I'ma make sure that he is there."

"Aiight."

I walked off, feeling the Desert Eagle weighing against the small of my back. I couldn't wait to handle this business and be done with it. I couldn't get Sodi off of my mind. Circled around the entire set up, making my rounds. I needed to know what I was dealing with. The place looked way too crowded. I got to wondering how many people were going to run in and out of the bathroom before I could do what I had to. Then, after I finished sending Blue on his way, I worried about getting away without anybody seeing me. That seemed next to impossible. Something told me to look over my shoulder. When I did, I saw Juelz jogging over to me. I stopped and waited for him.

He stopped directly in front of me, breathing hard. "Bruh, abort this mission. This nigga ain't down here. He stayed back in a lil' shack about twenty minutes from here. Sodi say he fucked up too. Now is the best time to catch his ass slipping. Come on."

***

Juelz stormed the Benz, pushing his foot hard on the gas. "Damn, Juelz, slow down. You gon' fuck around and get us pulled over, and I know you don't wanna be locked up in a Jamaican jail. They don't feed you in them ma'fuckas!" Sodi hollered.

"Bitch, shut up. We gotta hit this nigga before he wake up out of his slumber. You say Tank gon' be here too?" He asked looking into the backseat at her.

She nodded. "Yep, both of they ass fucked up on that Lean. They just called one of his men to go and pick him up some powder so it could wake him up. Tank saying he can't perform under those conditions. And Blue saying he can't manage that way either."

Juelz looked over at me. "That's all I'm talking about." He switched gears, and stepped on the gas, flying full speed down the highway. The Benz jerked and shot forward like a bullet.

Something didn't seem right to me. It just seemed a lil' fishy that Sodi had all of this information, yet she was still at the album release party waiting on Juelz to get there. I didn't know what she had against Blue, but it was obvious that she hated him. Then, when it came to Blue how could he not know that the female he was dealing with was up to no good? I mean, he had brought her all the way out to Jamaica. They had to be some sort of close.

"Baby, make sure you kill his ass dead, too. That nigga been talking hella crazy about what he gon' do when he see you." She added.

"Bitch, I don't get involved in all that baby daddy drama. This nigga was a job to me. That's it." He made a hard left and stepped on his gas again.

"Whatever. I was just telling you." She crossed her arms and looked out of the window.

We pulled up to the road that Blue's shack was supposed to be on. Juelz decreased his speed and floated down the road. "Which one of these fucked up shacks is it? They all look alike." He looked from the right side of the road, and then to the left.

"It's a bit of a ways up. You gon' see it in a minute. It got a Rolls Royce parked right inside the homemade dirt driveway. It's his uncle's."

"Aiight, bet." Juelz sounded focused. "I'm finna set Kingston on fire." He growled through clenched teeth.

My phone buzzed. I looked at the face, and my heart dropped into my chest. There was a message from Punkin that read: *"It's Sodi. You need to get home. I swear I didn't have nothing to do with it."* My eyes got bucked.

Juelz turned onto the dirt driveway right behind the Rolls Royce and jumped out of it with the Tech .9 already in his hand. He cocked it. "Come on, bruh, let's holler at this nigga right now." Then he was rushing up to it with Sodi leading the way.

Chapter 3

I sat there looking at the face of my phone, wondering if I should call Sodi. But as I glanced of out the window I saw that Juelz was already seconds away from stepping up to the door of the shack where Blue and Tank were supposed to be. He stopped and looked back. When he saw that I was still sitting in the car he threw his arms up. I threw the phone on the back seat, and slid out of the car with the silenced Desert Eagle in the small of my back. Juelz came partway down the dirt driveway with his arms still held out at his sides.

I rushed to him. "Dawg, we gotta hurry this shit up. Somethin' wrong with Sodi. I just got a call from Punkin. She ain't say exactly what's good, but I can tell that somethin' is wrong."

Juelz frowned at me. He leaned in close to my left ear. "Nigga, that shit gon' have to wait. We already here. We gotta finish this mission, and then we'll be able to take care of the home front. That's just what it is. Now come on." He headed toward the front door of the shack where Sodi stood with a key in her hand.

I shook my head, and followed behind him, vexed. I couldn't get the thought of what the problem could've been back home out of my head. I was praying that my woman was good. She had already been through a lot with the loss of her brother Roberto less than a week prior. I stepped in front of the door, beside both Juelz and Sodi.

Sodi took a deep breath, and slowly turned the key in the lock. She eased it open. Then took a step back. I could see that she was nervous, and a bit of excited.

Juelz stepped into the shack first. He upped two Glocks, and a serious mug came across his face. He waved for me to follow him.

Tired of being the one given orders, I brushed past him and rushed into the shack. There was a strong odor of fish and cigarette smoke. The lights were dimmed on the inside. Somewhere close I could hear Reggae music playing. My eyes scanned the interiors quick. The door opened to a small room. There was a wooden table that had syringes, and a brown powder like substance beside them. There was a bottle of champagne, and a six pack of beer. I moved further inside with my finger on the trigger of the silenced Desert Eagle, ready to squeeze it if anything out of the ordinary jumped out at me. More images of Sodi ran through my mind causing my anxiety to go through the roof. I moved through that room and entered into a bigger living room type of space. This one had a big wooden table. On top of the table were all kinds of assault rifles, and green boxes of ammunition. Seeing it made my stomach turn over. Now I was in panic mode.

Juelz rushed in front of me into that room, and further past it. When he got to the kitchen before I could get there, he jumped back, and upped his gun. His eyes were low. He pulled on the trigger, yet it refused to discharge. He fell to the floor, still trying to squeeze it.

I heard the squeaking of shoes on the linoleum. A door opened and crashed into a wall. Next I was inside of the kitchen. I looked to my left, and saw Blue grabbing a shotgun out of the cabinet to the left of him. He pumped it and got ready to aim it at Juelz. Before he could get it into position, I fired back to back. The gun jumped in my hand spitting fire.

Blue jerked his head back twice as the bullets smashed into his face, knocking double holes inside of it. The shotgun he was holding went off. He fell to his knees face-first. His brain made a mess on the floor. Steam coming off of it.

Juelz jumped up. His eyes were big. He looked at the Glocks in his hand. "Fuck, man. I forgot to load these mafuckas, bruh. I just fucking forgot." He said with sweat pouring down his face.

"Juelz! Tank just ran out the side door to the shack! He on his way down the—"

Boom! Boom! Boom!

Sodi screamed. Then I heard a loud thumping sound as if something had fallen to the dirt hard. We both rushed to the front of the shack. Sodi lay on her side with two massive holes in her chest. She struggled to breathe. Her eyes were bucked wide open. Juelz stopped, and kneeled beside her. I took off running behind Tank.

Tank hit the main road and got to running full speed. He was running so fast that all I could make out was the dust coming from under his shoes. I tried my best to cover most of the distance that he had gotten. He stopped and turned around. Aimed his pistol, and finger fucked it back to back. *Boom! Boom! Boom! Boom!*

I fell on my stomach. Waited for him to stop shooting, before I jumped up and took off running behind him again. I aimed and fired over and over. He kept running. I kept chasing him. I could feel rocks and gravel under my feet. The further I ran down the road after him, the darker it got. My chest began to hurt. My lungs felt like they were being ripped out of me. I had to stop. That ma'fucka was way too fast for me to catch. I stopped and turned around. Every few paces I would look over my shoulder to see where he was until he disappeared from my view altogether.

When I got a quarter of the way back to the shack all of the sudden about fifty Jamaicans stepped out of the darkness and blocked my path on the dirt road. Their long dreads hung in front of them like wool ropes. One in particular, a heavyset dark skinned man, stood in the very front of the pack with an AK47 in his hand. Behind him every last one of the members in his group were carrying pistols from .22s to AK47s.

I stopped and looked back over my shoulder. I thought about making a run for it. I thought about bussing at them and hitting as many as I could while I made my retreat, but I knew it would've been pointless. So, I kept walking right until I was standing a few feet in front of the man I assumed to be the leader.

He had his head slightly lowered with his red eyes pinned on me. "Ya' from 'round here, Boy?"

I shook my head. "N'all, homie. Just had a lil' situation wit' one of the niggas that was hiding out down here."

He sucked his teeth and frowned. "Ya' come to this corner of Kingston piping ya' gun not knowing that it kin cost you 'er life. Ya' see, me run dese here parts, Boy. Ya' don't run a damn ting." He aimed his assault rifle at me. And since he did, every nigga standing out there did.

I froze. I knew it was over. My heart got to pounding in my chest. Sodi crossed my mind. Then Punkin. I got to hating Juelz for convincing me to even leave Chicago. I didn't know shit about other cities or other places on earth, but I knew Chicago. That was my homeland. I was supposed to die there. Not in some fucking Jamaica.

The leader must've seen the worry on my face because he got to laughing. That made me feel like a bitch. I tightened up my manly right away. Wasn't nobody finna kill me while I felt I was in a state of being a pussy. "What's da matter, Boy? You look like you seen a ghost?" He started laughing again.

I mugged him. "Nigga, fuck you. I ain't seen shit. I told you what my business was. You aiming all dese ma'fuckin' guns at me and shit. If you gon' pull dem triggers, pull dem ma'fuckas. Ain't no hoes over here."

His eyes got big. He smiled and looked back at his crew. "We got a tough Bumbaclot Rude Boy here, yeah. Okay." He turned back to me with an angry mug on his face. I knew it was over.

Beep! Beep! Beep! Beep! The entire crowd turned around to see Juelz flying down the dirt road inside of the Benz. When he got closer to them he stepped on the gas, running down at least ten of the shooters. The Benz looked as if it was rolling over big rocks. The men hollered and screamed. The rest ran for cover. Juelz slammed on the brakes in front of me and threw open the passenger's door.

I jumped inside just as the shooting started. The back window exploded. Then the sides. The car began to shake as more and more bullets rocked its foundation. "Nigga, pull off! Fuck is you waiting on?" I hollered.

He stepped on the gas, and the car lurched forward. "Who da fuck is them niggas?" He asked with blood all over his face.

"Nigga, I don't know, but drive this ma'fucka!" I ducked as low in my seat as I could. The bullets kept coming. I said a silent prayer in my head asking God to please allow for us to get the fuck off of that island in one piece.

Juelz made a hard left. The car fishtailed. He slammed on the brakes and waited until the car straightened out. Then he stepped on the gas again. He wiped blood off of his face. "That bitch dead, bruh. That nigga killed her ass."

I nodded. "I know, nigga. We gotta get the fuck out of here. You need to slow this ma'fucka down now before we get pulled over."

"I had a thing for shorty, man. I mean, I didn't love that bitch or nothing. But I definitely had a thing for her. What the fuck am I gon' tell my son how his mother died when he get older?" He asked me. He seemed like he was almost in a panic state. I had never seen him act like he was acting before.

I shrugged. "You got plenty time to figure that shit out. For now, we need to be focusing on getting up off this punk ass island before them dread heads kill us."

He wiped a lone tear from his eye. "Yeah, you right. Plus, fuck that bitch. We all gotta die sooner or later. Shit, she got what she had coming I guess. Fuck that bitch!" He said the phrase again as if he was trying to convince himself that it was how he really felt.

I climbed up to the passenger's seat and looked out of the back window. There didn't seem to be an enemy in sight. I breathed a sigh of relief. "Look, bruh, as soon as we get back to this hotel, we finna tell Jackie that we need to jump on a plane tonight. Fuck later."

"Nigga, we can't leave tonight. I still got one more move that gotta be fulfilled before we leave the island. You already know that ain't how this game go. Plus, that nigga, Tank gotta—"

I thought my eyes were playing tricks on me at first. I squinted, and sure enough Tank came into view. He was walking along another dirt road. He stopped to light a cigarette, and kept it moving. My hearing seemed to have shut off while I was processing everything. When I came to, Juelz was asking me if I agreed with him. I continued to ignore him. "Nigga, stop the car."

"What?"

"Bruh, stop the car, and let me out." I ordered, with the passenger's door already slightly ajar.

He mugged me but stopped the car. "Fuck is you on?"

I jumped out of the car and took off running full speed with the Desert Eagle in my hand. I could feel my shoes kicking up rocks as I ran. Up ahead, Tank continued to walk leisurely down the road as if he didn't have a care in the world. When I was close enough to feel comfortable that I would get a good shot, I stopped and aimed with one eye closed. *Boof! Boof!* The silenced Desert Eagle jumped in my hand, and spat two bullets in the air.

Tank lunged forward, and fell. He got back up, and looked at me running toward him. He took off running again, but this time he was missing a step. He turned around and pulled out his gun. I fired four times, hitting him up before he could fire once. He dropped the gun and fell to his knees. Then I was standing over him.

Juelz pulled the Benz up, and jumped out. He picked up Tank's gun and cocked it just as it began to pour down raining. "You bitch ass nigga, you killed my baby mother." He raised his Jordan, and stomped Tank in the face over and over again. Tank groaned and yelped in pain. Juelz kept stomping. Then he fell to his knees and proceeded to beat him senselessly with the handle of his own gun. When Juelz stood back up, Tank's face had been caved in with his noodles leaking out of his forehead.

"Aiight, nigga, let's get the fuck out of here!" I hollered, pulling on his shirt.

Juelz fired four rounds into the already deceased Tank. Stood looking down on him for what felt like a million years. Then he ran to the car and pulled off.

***

Back at the hotel Jackie was livid. "Y'all had me pay all of this fuckin' money so I could enjoy a weekend with the two of you, and now y'all saying that you want me to leave early? What type of shit is that?"

Juelz was out handling his business. I didn't really give a fuck what Jackie was talking about. I'd hit Punkin up ten times and she hadn't got back to me. Neither had Sodi. I was so worried that I was losing my mind. "Look, Jackie, I done already told yo ass what it was. Now pack yo shit so we can get the fuck up out of here. You costing me some valuable time."

"I'm costing you what?" She spat. "Nigga, you ain't nothing but a motherfucking dope boy. You ain't got no time, or no real money, so I don't wanna hear none of that shit. Do you hear me?"

I mugged her for a second. Then kept packing. She had my temper as hot as a burning charcoal. I couldn't feed into her bullshit.

"Did you hear what I said TJ?" She asked screaming.

That did it. I jumped up and grabbed her by the throat. Slammed her ass into the wall and squeezed my big hand around her neck. "Bitch, I heard you, but did you hear me? Huh?"

She slapped at my hand. Her eyes were as big as pool balls. Tears dripped down her cheeks. She kept gagging.

I squeezed as hard as I could and dropped her ass. "Get yo monkey ass over there and pack yo shit. We leaving this bitch first thing in the morning. That's it."

She sat on the floor looking up at me. "I hate you, lil' boy!" She came to her feet. "I don't know what has gotten into you, but I hate your fucking guts!"

I didn't care how she felt. I had Sodi on my mind. I needed to get home to her. The fear of the unknown was killing me.

Chapter 4

As soon as my feet stepped into the parking lot of O'Hare Airport, Punkin pulled up alongside me and Juelz. She hopped out with a stressed look on her face. There appeared to be bags under her eyes. It was a windy day. Very cloudy. I could tell that it had been raining a lot. The pavement was wet, and the scent of rain was heavy in the atmosphere. Punkin rushed to me and wrapped her arms around my neck. "We gotta get to the hospital right now. Maybe if Sodi can hear your voice she can pull through."

My heart dropped. "Pull through? What the fuck do you mean pull through?" I asked, already feeling like I was about to lose my mind.

Punkin backed away and lowered her head. "Her house was robbed, TJ. I don't really know what all happened, but she was shot five times. The house was ransacked, and supposedly Roberto had left her plenty dope or whatever. Somebody must've known about it because they came and got it. They tried killing her in the process. At least that's the story that I am being told by her mother, and some of her family. But come on, we gotta go now."

I looked over to Juelz, he looked equally sick. He swallowed his spit. "Dawg, what you wanna do?" He came around to stand on the side of me.

My temper felt like it was about to explode. I got dizzy. "Ain't shit we can do other than find out who the fuck did this shit. Come on, let's ride out and go see her."

"Unfortunately, I'ma have to meet you there. I gotta check in with a few people so I can let you know that all of the tasks have been complete. Then I'll be there to support you, homie. You already know that." He pat me on the back. "Say, Punkin, where are they holding her at?"

"She's at Chicago Medical."

"Aiight, TJ, I'ma meet you there in a few hours. Hold ya' head, my dude." He slid his arm around Jackie's neck. She refused to make eye contact with me.

I nodded. "Yep." On some real shit, I didn't know what I was about to walk into. I felt like I needed Juelz by my side. He would stop me from becoming too emotional over the state I was sure I was going to find Sodi in. I slid into Punkin's whip, as I watched him and Jackie walk off. "Aiight, Ma, let's ride out."

She placed her hand on top of mine and squeezed it. "TJ, I just want you to know that I love you, and I got your back. Please just know that. Okay?"

"Yo, pull off, Punkin. I need to see my shorty." I didn't feel like going there emotionally with her. I had a bunch of devious shit running through my brain. A man never really understands how much a woman means to him until something happens to her that he wishes he could've prevented. This is how I was feeling about Sodi. I was wishing that I had never went to Jamaica. Had I not, I honestly felt like I could've prevented anything from happening to my first love.

Punkin pulled off. She looked angry. "Look, I understand that you're mad about what happened to

Sodi, but I'm still here. I'm still present for you, and I am still pregnant with our child. Have you even worried about my physical wellbeing while you were in Jamaica?"

"Punkin, on some real shit, if you make me do this shit right now, you're not going to like the responses you get from me. I swear to Jehovah you want. Now is not the time for you to make shit about you. So shut the fuck up and drive until I find out what happened to my woman. Can you do that?"

She tightened her lips and looked out at the parking lot through her windshield. "Aiight, TJ, I got you. But after you see what's up with her, it's my turn. You understand that?"

I ignored her and drifted off into the deepest recesses of my thoughts. I missed my mother. I also missed my sister Marie. Both had been taken way too soon. I felt like Sodi had been the only one in this world that loved me as much as they had. If she suddenly passed way, I didn't know what I was going to do.

***

I asked Punkin to let me visit Sodi alone. I didn't know how seeing her was going to make me respond, and I wasn't comfortable with crying in front of anybody, especially not Punkin. I was sure that she would be even more jealous of Sodi than she already was. So, she granted me this wish and promised to wait in the lobby for me.

I stepped into her room in the Intensive Care Unit an hour later. I wasn't past the doorway before tears fell down my cheeks. Sodi was hooked up to so many machines that I just knew it was over for her. I made my way to her bedside on wobbly knees. She had a breathing tube down her throat. There were all kinds of IVs in the back of her hands. I saw a feeding tube as well. Her eyes were closed. She looked smaller already. Her skin looked paler. The right side of her face was covered by patches that were drenched in blood. The right side of her face also looked caved in closer to her forehead. I buckled and fell to my knees. The sight was too much. How the fuck could this shit have happened to my baby, is all I kept thinking. I broke down with tears coming worse than they ever had. I was crying so hard that I didn't even notice that there was somebody else in the room until I felt a warm hand on the back of my neck. This made me jump up, defensive. "Punkin, I told yo ass to wait in the lobby." I snapped. Then stopped when I saw that it wasn't her, but a familiar face none the less.

Jelissa held her hands up. "Whoa, TJ, I did not expect for you to react like that. I'm sorry for invading your space. I just thought you needed a comforting hand."

I continued looking her over. It was taking me a second to honestly remember who she was. My brain was drawing a blank. I wiped the tears from my face. "You look familiar."

She smiled. "Boy, I know yo memory ain't that bad. You don't remember barging into my house on the south-eastside with your guy Juelz, looking for Deion?"

I thought about it for a minute. "What's your name? That'll help me."

"Jelissa. Remember, me and Deion had a thing, before he beat me into the ground?"

It came to me right away after she said those last words. "Aw, yeah. I remember. What's good wit' you? Why are you here?" Jelissa was five feet four inches tall. Caramel skinned, with pure brown eyes. She had natural curly hair, with light freckles that made her look real gorgeous to me. Her eyes were almond slanted. She was slim up top but slim-thick down low. I remembered her having a fat ass that caught me off guard because the rest of her seemed so slim. "Sodi is my homegirl. She was the only real friend I had."

"Have." I corrected her.

"Oops, I'm sorry. You're right. Have." She walked over to Sodi, and ran her fingers through her hair. "She is so beautiful. I can't believe that anybody would do this to her." She whispered.

I came and stood over my woman. I could smell Jelissa's perfume from where I stood. She smelled good. I liked that. "When I find out who did this to my baby, they gon' pay. I ain't gon' have no mercy on they bitch ass." Another tear seeped out of my eye.

Jelissa nodded in understanding. "You really love her don't you?"

"Yeah." Now both eyes were leaking. "Sodi is my heart. She the only person I got left on this earth that actually give a genuine fuck about me. If she die, man, this world gon' feel my wrath. I swear that to Jehovah, man."

Jelissa kissed Sodi on the side of her forehead that wasn't caved in. "Well, hopefully she doesn't pass away. She's a fighter. But even if she does, I'm sure that she isn't the only person in the world that loves you."

I nodded. "Yes, she is. But I ain't finna get into all of that shit wit' you, Shorty. I don't even know yo ass like that."

She smiled at me again, showcasing her dimples. "That's understandable. I'm a real secretive person too. I didn't mean to overstep my bounds."

"What did you hear happened to her?" I asked, looking Sodi over. She looked like she was in some serious pain. I wished that I could've been her sacrifice. I wished that I had never gone to Jamaica. I hated myself.

"Somebody knew that Roberto had left Sodi a bunch of money and dope. She was on the phone with me when Emilio dropped it off to her a day before he had been killed for the same stuff that he had given his sister. Something ain't right, and I honestly don't know what to think." She kissed Sodi again.

"I thought Roberto was killed because somebody was trying to rob him?"

"He was, but now I'm finding out that before Roberto was killed, he and one of his guys had ripped off some Cartel dudes. Apparently, they were dead-set on getting back what he had taken from them, so I won't really call it a robbery that they committed because they were shaking him down for their stuff. However, when Roberto wouldn't tell them where their merch was he was killed."

"Damn." I felt sick. "So, they took what he did out on Sodi?"

Jelissa nodded. "I guess so. But then again, they are saying that they hit up Sodi's crib at like four in the morning. They probably found out that she was holding dude's merchandise, came to get it, and Sodi wasn't going. Then they shot her up, but she got some shots off as well. They found another person's blood at the scene and supposedly they are out looking for him. But you already know how Chicago is. They'll say they looking, but actually doing it is another story." She exhaled, rubbing Sodi's long, curly hair.

I stood there trying to piece together everything that she told me. "You been knowing Sodi for a while right?"

She nodded. "Since we were kids. Her mother used to allow for me to spend my summers down here in Chicago after we moved away, and in return my mother would let her come and stay with us in Newark, New Jersey for every other summer. Our families would alternate."

"That's cool, but I got a question. How close is this Emilio mafucka to the family?"

"He is Roberto's best friend. When we first moved down to Chicago when I was eleven years old, Emilio and Roberto were already best friends. They did everything together just like me and Sodi did. Why do you ask me that?"

"Because, it seem like he's an important piece of the puzzle. Do you have any idea which one of Roberto's friends that he hit the lick on the Cartel with?"

"No. I'm sorry, I don't."

"But if you had to guess, who would you say it was?"

"Uh." She ran her fingers through her hair. "Roberto was a real lonesome person. The only one I have ever seen him really jamming with was Emilio. They were like two peas in a pod. So, if I had to say anybody it would most definitely be him."

"My point exactly. I need to holler at that nigga. Where do I find him?"

Jelissa looked a bit worried. "TJ, I know you get down in these streets, but you don't wanna just run up on Emilio asking him questions about Roberto's death, especially if you're going to do it in an accusatory fashion. You'll make an enemy instead of a friend."

"What, man? Bitch, I don't give a fuck about making no enemy. My muthafuckin' woman is laying in a hospital bed, barely hanging on to life. You think I give a fuck about Emilio?"

She exhaled slowly and stepped back from Sodi. "Uh, I know you going through some things and all of that, but you're not going to disrespect me by calling me an animal that walks on four legs. My name is Jelissa. If that's to long for you to pronounce, you can call me Lisa, or Queen. Other than that, this ain't gon' work out. I'm letting you know that right now."

I looked at this bitch like she was crazy. "Shorty, fuck what you talking 'bout. This is Chicago. In Chicago, we call hoes bitches. That's just what it is. Now, anyway, do you know where I can get in touch with Emilio? Yes or no?"

"N'all, bitch. I don't." She snapped.

"What?" I made a move toward her.

She held her ground. "I don't know what you thought this was, but I am not afraid of you. You better ask somebody. I am a strong woman. If you think you gon' disrespect me and I don't return that to you, then you have another thing coming."

A nurse stepped into the room with a chart in her hand. She headed over to Sodi's monitors and started to write things down. She smiled at both me and Jelissa as we mugged each other in silence. We waited for her to leave the room and close the door.

"Seriously, TJ, we have to be more mature than what we were a few moments ago. I apologize for calling you a bitch. That ain't even how I get down. I got more respect for myself than that. Secondly, I lied to you about Emilio. I know where to find him."

I stepped closer to Sodi and kissed her cheeks. "That's my bad, too. I shouldn't have called you out of your name. That was foul. I ain't think yo lil' ass was gon' say shit though."

"Now you know." She rolled her eyes. "Anyway, Emilio kicks it over in Humboldt Park on the westside of the city. He calls for the Kings over there now that Roberto is out of the picture. You have to be careful though. He got a death squad running under him and all of them are trigger happy."

I didn't give a fuck about none of that. They was gon' have to kill me. It was as simple as that. Emilio needed to convince me that he didn't have shit to do with Sodi getting hit up. If he couldn't, I was finna be at his head like a bullet and a dome shot. "What made you lie to me about it in the first place?"

She took a deep breath and looked down at Sodi. "I know how much you mean to Sodi. I guess I just didn't want to put you in harm's way. It would suck if both of you were laid up like this." She laid her cheek against hers. "But I wish you the best. She already told me how you get down, and I know I can't stop you."

"Hell n'all, you can't." I kissed Sodi on the lips simultaneously. I couldn't kiss them both because of the tubes going down her throat. After I finished, I hopped up and headed toward the door to the hospital.

"Wait!" Jelissa called. She caught up to me and looked up. "I never did get a chance to thank you for giving me a safe place to refuge after Deion did what he did to me. That meant a lot. I owe you."

I waved her off. "Don't mention it, Shorty. It's good." I pulled her to me and hugged her. "Just make sure that my woman is good. I'll be back once I straighten some things out in the street."

"Will do." She gave me a salute and headed back to Sodi. My eyes unintentionally trailed down to her jiggling ass. I watched it for a few seconds before I had to snap out of the trance. Then I left the room feeling guilty.

46

Chapter 5

A week later me and Punkin were coming from the doctor's office, on the way to her Benz truck, when she stopped in the middle of the parking lot and crossed her arms. I'd spent the entire week prior looking for Emilio. No matter how many times I rolled out to the westside of Chicago asking around from him nobody seemed to know where he was. Often times the people I asked would just mug me with hatred in their eyes. I was irritated, and feeling like a complete loser.

I turned around, and looked to Punkin. "Shorty, what's good with you?" It was two in the afternoon. The sun was shining, and there was a slight breeze. I had on a pair of Chanel sunglasses because I was feeling real sick over Sodi. Jelissa told me she was getting worse. They rushed her into surgery as recent as that morning and weren't allowing for any visitors to be in there with her. On top of that, the police were all over the lobby looking to ask her supporters for clues in the case. But they were also on some slick shit, running everybody's names and locking up those that had warrants. Sometimes I hated Chicago.

"What is the matter with you now, TJ? We just got some really good news that we are having a son. And he's healthy in there. Why didn't that put a smile on your face?" She asked.

I scanned the lot and saw two squad cars roaming through it. "Yo, let's just get in your truck and we'll talk about this shit in there. Come on."

She followed my gaze and spotted the two squad cars as well. "Yeah, okay, but we better talk about it, too." She chirped her alarm and popped the doors.

I pulled mine open and slid into the passenger's seat as low as I could without making it look to obvious. It seemed like Punkin was taking her time although I might've been being a bit insensitive due to the fact that she was pregnant. By the time she got inside of the truck I was so irritated that I was ready to argue. A squad car slowly cruised past her truck. She started the ignition and got to rubbernecking to see what the police were doing.

"Man, just pull da fuck off. Damn, you acting like you want them to pull us over or something."

"Nigga, shut up!" She snapped. "Damn. You always talking crazy. If you wanted me to get out of here faster, then you should've been gentlemen enough to open my door for me." She curled her upper lip and pulled off.

I stared at her, super annoyed. "Yo, I swear, I don't see how the fuck I been obsessed wit' yo ass since we was shorties. I guess I didn't know that you was this mafuckin' annoying."

"What? Boy, please. You annoying as hell too. You think the whole fuckin' world is supposed to just stop running all because you're going through somethin'. That ain't how it works."

"Yeah, whatever."

"Anyway, so why you ain't get out of your funky mood when you found out that we were having a boy, and that he is healthy so far?" She asked, cruising on to the expressway.

"I don't know. I guess I got Sodi on my mind like crazy. Jelissa said she getting worse. They got so many police swarming around that mafucka that I can't even get in there to see her. I feel like shit. I should be there supporting her like she did me when I was on lock."

Punkin drove for a minute in silence. "Yeah, you should. But at the same time, you just said that a bunch of police are swarming all around the hospital, right?"

"Yeah, they on that bitch shit. Been taking cats to jail for their warrants and all type of shit."

"Alright then. If all of that is going on, then it would be stupid of you to be there. You already know that there is a chance that they gon' lock you back up."

"Yeah, it is, but then again, I don't really know."

"Are you willing to take that risk?" She asked, looking over to me?

I shook my head. "I ain't going back to nobody's prison. They gon' have to kill me first. Word to God."

"Don't talk like that. You got a whole ass son on the way. You have to be smarter about things than you have been this far."

"Shut the fuck up. I already know that. Yo, I swear you think you my mother or something."

"No, I don't, and what would even make you say some weird shit like that?"

"Because, you always trying to scold me for some shit like I'ma lil' kid or something." I pulled out a stuffed Garcia Vega. Green Leaf. Sparked that bitch. A thick cloud of smoke entered into the truck.

Punkin frowned. "Boy, do you want your son having asthma?"

"Nah. Why would you ask me that?" I took five strong pulls and inhaled them deeply. I needed to be lifted. Punkin was getting on my nerves.

"Because, you sitting in here with the windows rolled up, smoking on a fat ass blunt like I ain't sitting over here super pregnant. That seems so negligent to me."

I exhaled the smoke. "You see what I mean? Shorty, you acting like a old ass woman." I let down my window just enough for the smoke to seep out of it.

"Well, one of us has to be mature in this whole thing. Once again, we are about to bring a child into the mix. Don't that mean anything to you?"

"Yeah, it mean you finna be getting on my mafuckin' nerves for the next eighteen years and three months." I joked. I was high as an airplane in flight. My eyelids were lower than a basement.

Punkin shook her head. "Boy, you ain't no good. I know you better get it together real fast though. This baby will be here in no time." She turned on the air conditioner.

I stubbed out the blunt. "Nah, on some real shit though. It felt good hearing that our kid is going to be healthy. That's what's up. And I know I been acting like a asshole to you lately. I just been going through it. I miss Sodi."

Punkin cringed. I caught that action. She turned to me with a fake smile on her face. "Look, TJ, I just gotta be woman about some stuff. I understand that you really love Sodi. I mean, that's cool and all, but I don't wanna hear about your love and missing of her every second that we are together. I need for you to miss me when you not with me. I need for you to focus some more on the fact that you are about to be a father. Let's get you passionate about those factors like you are about your precious Sodi."

I shot her an angry glance. "What you say?"

She kept rolling. The L-Train stormed past on its tracks, screeching loudly while we drove alongside its barriers on the freeway. She stepped on the gas and pushed the speedometer to ninety. The L-Train quickly became a part of our rearview mirrors. "I'm sorry for that last comment. Chop that up to the hormones."

I couldn't even be mad at her. I had been throwing me and Sodi's love for one another in her face a lot. I wasn't doing it on purpose. I just missed her so much. I didn't feel right about being with Punkin. I felt like I should've been right beside Sodi in that hospital room. Had I never gone to Jamaica she would've never been there in the first place. "Look, I apologize. I ain't mean to keeping throwing her in your face like that. That's bogus. From now on when I do, just give me a crazy look? That'll be my way to know that I'm doing too much. Aiight?"

She smiled. "Yeah, we'll see how good that works out for me. You just acting like it's good because you're high. Maybe I should encourage you to stay chopped all the time." She snickered.

I laughed. "So, how are we going to raise this boy?"

Her face got serious quick. "I already told you what I wanted to do. I want to insure that our child has the brightest chances of surviving in this day and age. The only way he can have the strongest chance is if he has the both of us under the same roof."

"So, you talking like you want us to be together?" I asked. I already knew that's what she wanted but I needed to hear her out anyway. I was trying to keep myself from talking because my every other thought was Sodi.

"Well, the more I think about it, I can't really see you settling down in some tamed stuff with me. It seem like you live to be on that wild boy stuff. That scares me, especially for our son's future."

"Yeah." I felt like shit.

"What have you done with the property that I gave you? Have you had anybody go over there to start to make repairs?" She asked, switching lanes.

I shook my head. "N'all, not yet. I been a bit preoccupied with everything that's been taking place. I guess I can jump on that starting tomorrow."

Her nostrils flared. "I hope you do. I mean, I know that you're sick because of what had happened to Sodi, but you can't allow for your whole life to shut down. If it is meant for her to make it, she will. If she doesn't, then that just means that God had another plan for her. A plan that we aren't at liberty to question." She kept looking down at her phone.

"Yeah, I guess. But I don't even wanna get to thinking like that. That type of thinking will only send me off. Straight up."

Punkin smiled weakly. "Well, baby, you may have too."

I frowned. "What?" My phone vibrated. I looked at the face. There was a text from Jelissa. It read: *TJ, Sodi passed away a half hour ago. I'm so sorry.* I dropped the phone and grabbed the blunt back out of the ashtray, sparking it. "Yo, don't say shit to me. Let's just roll around the city for a few hours while I take all of this in."

"Okay, baby. But just know that I'm here. If you wanna—"

"Punkin! Silence! Please!"

She placed her hand in front of her mouth and nodded. "Cool."

***

I argued with Sodi's mother for three days straight about giving my baby a proper funeral. She refused. Instead of her giving her a funeral she had her cremated and didn't even tell me when the ceremony was to take place. By the time I found out about it, it was all over and done with. I was sick.

I found myself blowing blunt after blunt. Drinking bottle after bottle of Patron until I would pass out. I couldn't keep no food down. I couldn't think straight either. My every other thought was of her. I shut my phone off and stayed held up in a seedy motel right off of Cottage Grove for a whole month and a half. That ma'fucka had big ass rats and roaches. I didn't give no fuck. I felt lower than them. Some days I wanted to die. I couldn't find any reason to live. I felt like my last and final purpose had gone and left me behind.

Forty-five days after I got to the motel, Jelissa talked me into letting her come out to see me. I don't know why I allowed her to. I guess it was because she was just as close to Sodi as I felt I was. Sodi had been her only friend for much of her life. I felt that she and I could connect over that.

She stepped into the motel room and saw that I had empty bottles of Patron everywhere. The floor was disgusting. Instead of using an ashtray, I had taken to dumping the ashes right on the carpet. Rats scurried around, eating the left-over food I had everywhere. She gasped at the conditions. "TJ, I know you're screwed up right now, but can we please spend some time at my place? Just until you can pull yourself together?"

I scratched my full beard. My dreads looked rough as a bitch too. There was a roach crawling down my arm that I didn't feel until it got to my wrist. I shook it off and didn't even manage to step on it. "Yeah, aiight, Shorty, but we can do that shit in the morning. I need one more day to myself, then I'll fuck wit' you. How does that sound?"

She looked around. "Yo, that sound cool. Just promise me that you gon' come?"

"I will."

"Aiight, I'ma see you in the morning then. I'll text you the address." She stepped forward and hugged me. "Whew! Boy, you rank."

I sniffed under my arm. I was banging. "Oh, well. Ain't nobody here but me."

She stepped forward and took my face into her little hands. "Listen to me, bro. You are stronger than this. You are a savage. All this, whatever this is, ain't you. All my girl used to talk about were the things that you came through when you were a kid, and while you were locked up. Don't have her looking down on you and seeing a wimp. Come on now." She kissed my cheek. "Get it together. I'll see you in the morning. Bank on it."

I nodded. "Aiight." Her words hit me like a ton of bricks. I felt horrible, and weak. I felt I was acting like a straight chump. I had to pick myself up. I just needed to release a few more tears, and then I was sure I would be good. I went back to the bed and laid down. Scrolling through pictures of Sodi and myself together. I laid there and I let out every ounce of emotion that I had pinned up inside of me. When it was all said done, I was ready to begin the next chapter without her physically in my life. I still felt broken, but after all of the tears, I was ready to at least try my luck at moving forward.

T.J. Edwards

Chapter 6

Jelissa was true to her word. She popped up at eight in the morning, rolling a black on black Range Rover Sport. Before she blew her horn three times I was already out the door, and standing in from of the rented room.

She hopped out of the big truck rocking a Fendi skirt that clung to her small frame. Her ass poked out like a pregnant belly. Her curly hair looked freshly whipped, and so were her nails. She stood smiling. The sun shimmering off of the sheen of her hair. "Yo, I told you I would be here at eight in the morning. I bet you thought I was playing, huh?"

I shook my head. "N'all, I didn't. You see me up, ready to go." I held my arms out.

She gave me a stank face as she looked me up and down. "Yo. Kid, don't tell me you still feeling real low? I mean, if you are, we can work on that today. But, damn you look rough."

I felt offended, but only for a second. "Yeah, I know. I gotta get myself together. Maybe swing by the mall or something."

She shook her head. "It's all good, bruh. Huh." She opened her arms, and walked toward me.

I looked at her like she was stupid. When she got close enough for us to hug I still kept my arms at my sides. "Nah. Shorty, you can't be taking digs at me, and then expect me to be all ready to hug on you and shit. That ain't how that go."

She crossed her arms in front of her small chest. "Oh, so now who getting all serious and stuff? I was just messing with you. But you do look rough as hell. I'm used to seeing you, the few times that I have seen you, all put together. Now you look a lil' rough, but I'm sure that you know." She giggled.

"Yo, fuck you, Jelissa. I'm 'bout to go back in here and chill. I'll get up with you at another time." I started back to the motel. I had some of that OG Kush straight from California, and I had plans on taking me a few blunts to the head. I ain't feel like dealing with shorty ass in that moment.

She rushed over and grabbed my arm. "TJ, wait."

I yanked my shit away from her. "What?" Now I was mugging her lil' fine ass and trying my best to not acknowledge how bad she was to me. Although she appeared to be all Black, she had a lot of Spanish features. Her nose. Her eyes. Her hair. She even had a Spanish figure that was so slim, yet thick at the same time. I might've been doing too much because it had been a few weeks since I'd actually gotten some pussy too. I think my nature might've been calling me.

"Look, I apologize. I just want you to roll with me for a few hours. Let me get you right. Besides, I wanna reminisce about Sodi. I got a surprise for you." She said, looking up to me with her soulful brown eyes.

I softened a bit. "Aiight, Shorty, but quit coming for a nigga unless you want me to clap back at yo lil' ass."

She laughed. "Dang, who would've ever though that yo killa ass was sensitive?" She quipped.

"Ain't shit sensitive about me. I just ain't feeling all the way right. That's all." I locked the motel door and climbed into her Range Rover. The inside had pink leather seats with her initials stitched into the headrest. "Damn. Shorty, how the fuck you rolling a Range?"

She waited until I closed the door before she pulled off. The automatic seatbelts locked around my chest. "What? You thought because I was a female that I wasn't chasing my bag a something?" She asked.

"N'all, I ain't saying that. I honestly didn't think that far into it. But what do you do though?"

She turned Jhenè Aiko on to the radio and got to bobbing her head to the music. "I'm a self-made entrepreneur. I have two beauty shops. One restaurant, and a few properties out in Harvey, Illinois, and Riverdale. I'm just trying to make my way out here until my real dream kicks off."

I was impressed. "Your real dream. What's that?"

She looked at me and smiled. "One day I'ma be a famous writer, and movie director. That's my dream."

I perked up at hearing the writing thing. "Yo, you fa real? You like to write?"

She nodded. "Yep. I got a few books that I wrote. I ain't tried to get nothing published yet. I need to edit them bad boys a lot." She placed a tuft of her curly hair behind her ears. She looked so fine from where I was sitting. I got to feeling all kinds of guilty. I knew that she was Sodi's best friend, and she'd once upon a time had something going with Deion. That part didn't bother me because I didn't give a fuck about that punk ass nigga. After all, as soon as I caught him, I was sure

I was gone knock his head off for putting Blue on my trail to murder me.

"Did Sodi tell you that I like to write too?" I asked, feeling her lil' swag. Every now and then her East Coast accent would slip out of her. It was sexy, and it was starting to make me feel some type of way about her. What way, I didn't know.

"She did more than that. She done let me read some of your short stories that you sent her while you were on lock. You got talent. I think you should go to school for it and really become a beast. That's what I'm doing online, and I gotta say that it has helped me to step my game all the way up."

That was something I would actually consider. There was nothing that I loved more in the world than writing. I had been through so much shit that I knew I could wrote for days and days and never get tired. "Yo, that shit you was saying about movies, that's my true passion, and what I ultimately wanna do. I think I got that sauce. Wait 'til my movies get on the big screen, I guarantee niggas gon' be feeling that shit to the fullest. I am the Trenches."

Jelissa kept rolling. "You gotta think bigger than the trenches though. That hood money only so much, whereas if you have that crossover appeal then you'll be able to run that check all the way up. You'll expand around the world."

"Yeah, that shit sound good, but before I do any thang I gotta put on for the slums. I'm always gon' be a street nigga. Fuck the globe. I'm from Chicago, Shorty. The Murder Capitol of the United States." I felt myself getting riled up. That hood shit beat deep in my heart and soul.

"Well, that's cool that you are so passionate about the slums the way that you are, but I'm telling you if you wanna be filthy rich, then you will force yourself to see outside of the hood."

"The hood is the only place where ma'fuckas gon' understand what I'm putting down. I can't write that soft, white shit. I can only write about the shit that I done been through and put it under the guise of fiction. But you best believe that my shit is really facts. I ain't no fiction type nigga."

"Yeah, I read a few of your stories, and I knew right then and there that you had some serious natural talent. But at the same time that you were missing a few screws up there." She laughed. "But, it's tough. If you could, where would you like to take your craft?"

I shrugged. "I don't know. Right now, I'm just trying to make it through today. Writing is the last thing on my mind, unfortunately, as much as I love it."

"Well I can understand that right now, but we gon' come back to it. You never know where that gift can take you." She sped through traffic, and got to taking side streets. "I hate traffic, so I'ma use a few shortcuts to get us back on the highway. We finna hit up Michigan Avenue so we can get you fitted. Then I'ma retwist your dreads for you while we sit back and chill. Like I said, I got a surprise for you." She smiled again. "For now, just sit back and relax."

I planned on doing exactly that, but first I had some questions for her. "Yo, didn't you have a son the last time I seen you?"

She nodded. "Yeah, his name is Rae'Jon. You remember him?"

"A lil' bit? I remember lil' homie did a lot of crying. He must've been going through something. Where is he now?"

"He's back home in New Jersey with my mother. I'm trying to establish myself out here for a short time before I bring him back. She has him in a really good school, so I'ma let him finish out the school year, and then we gon' move back to Chicago."

"That's what's up. You been fuckin wit' Deion at all?" I wanted to know because if she did I was sure that she would know where to find him. If I could get that out of her then it would make my job ten times easier.

"N'all, I ain't seen him in a few months now. The last time I did, things didn't go so good." She started to look sick in the face.

"Damn, it was that bad?"

She nodded. "Yeah, Deion got a habit of putting his hands on me. I really don't wanna talk about it though. I just wanna chill wit' you and get you up to par. Sodi would have wanted that."

At the mentioning of Sodi's name I felt sick on the stomach. I couldn't get her out of my system no matter how hard I tried. "Yo, I'm sorry for bringing dude ass up. I should've already known that it was going to leave a bad taste in your mouth. Every time I speak on him that shit get me so vexed that I can't see straight."

Jelissa smiled in understanding. "Yeah, I heard about what happened to Marie. I'm so sorry for your loss. Did you ever really get down to the nitty gritty of who did what?" She asked softly.

"How the fuck do you know about that?" I asked, shocked that she would even bring my sister's murder up.

"I didn't mean to offend you. Sodi was my best friend. There was very little that she didn't tell me. She felt just as bad about what happened to Marie as anybody else did. Not you of course because that was your little sister. But trust me, she felt terrible. Deion and all of them are some sick bastards. That's why I keep my distance from him."

I really started to feel sick once I got to thinking about how I lost Marie, and now Sodi. I felt like I needed to get high again, even though my high from earlier was still on full force. "You know what, how about we just talk about anything else but all of the bullshit that's been going on around us. I hear that you own two salons."

She smiled, showcasing both dimples on her cheeks. "Yes, I do. I never wanted to work under no one, nor answer to anyone. My dad died when I was sixteen. He left me a nice chunk of change and I used it to open my salons. Plus, I like to make money. Being broke ain't cute. Plus, I want better for myself, and my children."

"That's definitely what's up. I wish I could think like you thinking. I got a son on the way and instead of me finding ways to leave the streets alone, I keep finding more ways to jump back into them. I'm all fucked up."

"It's good though, TJ, you gotta crawl before you walk. You ain't never had no real role models. Ain't nobody ever showed you a better way than what you're already doing. That's the only reason you are how you are."

"That, and I got a bunch of niggas that done my people wrong. I can't ever live with myself until them niggas are six feet under. I'm just being honest."

"Shoot, you feel how you feel. That killa stuff is embedded deep within your soul. All I can say right now is that I will never judge you, and that I want us to be cool. I feel like we can help each other."

"How so?"

She shrugged. "Only time will tell, but I do know that we owe it to Sodi." She smiled at me and looked super gorgeous with her lil' baby hairs along her edges.

***

True to her word, Jelissa got me right. She took me to Michigan Avenue and bought me a Supreme fit, with the matching Balenciaga's. Next was the barbershop where I got my lining edged up. After the barbershop we headed off to her place where I showered, and then she sat me down between those sexy thighs and tightened up my dreads. After the whole time I sat there, I'm embarrassed admit I was on brick. I felt like I could smell a hint of her cat but I might've been psyching myself out. It had been way too long since I'd gotten some I suppose.

After she finished my hair she stood up and dusted herself off. She looked down at me and smiled. "Now that's the man that I remembered meeting back then. I'll be right back."

She left the room while I looked myself over in the mirror she'd handed me. She had me right. When she came back she had tears running down her cheeks. She stepped up to me and handed me a golden urn. "Here you go, TJ. Sodi would've wanted you to have this." She slumped to her knees and broke down crying her eyes out.

I accepted the urn, then fell down beside her. My throat was tight. I pulled her into my embrace, and kissed her forehead, resting my lips against them. "It's gon' be awright, Jelissa. We gon' get through this shit together."

T.J. Edwards

Chapter 7

"Yo, so who the hell is this broad again? Refresh my memory." Juelz said, blowing a big cloud of smoke out of his mouth. The smoke hit the windshield of his Benz, and permeated all around the car. I hadn't even had the chance to take a pull off of it, but I felt a contact almost immediately.

"She used to fuck wit' Deion back in the day. Remember the time we went out east, and Deion and JD came through? We had to rough them niggas up and all of that? The police came, and wound up snatching me up?"

Juelz kept rolling, but he was looking at the ceiling of the car from time to time like he was a damn fool. I could tell that he didn't know what the fuck I was talking about. But he nodded anyway.

"Remember I was telling you about the lil' bitch that held her own when the police tried to get her to roll over on us?" I was starting to get irritated.

He finally shook his head. "Nigga, my shit fried. My short and long term memory is popped. It is what it is though. I don't know who this bitch is but if she got you putting your phone on Do Not Disturb already, a mafucka in trouble." He handed me the blunt. "What's good with her though? You smash?"

"N'all, I ain't even try. I ain't on that with her. All we got in common in Sodi. Whenever I get to feeling like I'm missing her too much, and I need somebody to talk to about her, I go and find her. It's been working out for me so far." I took two strong pulls of the Kush and inhaled it deeply. I felt the burn I was looking for before I blew the smoke back out.

"What? That's how you feel? Why you ain't come and holler at me? You know I'll hold you down and go there with you." Juelz said busting up laughing. "Damn, dawg, that's fucked up. I couldn't even get that shit out without laughing. N'all, but that's cool though. If shorty somebody you can there with you need to keep her close. I mean sooner or later you gon' be tapping that ass anyway, but for now just focus on whatever she doing to keep your head in in the game."

"Right, that's exactly what I'ma do. I still about Sodi. I gotta find a way to move on though. Thoughts of her ain't healthy for me right now."

"I thought we was gon' slide on that Emilio nigga. What? You had a change of heart or something?" Juelz looked over at me.

I shook my head. "Never, I'm just waiting for the right time. It seem like every time I go over there I can never find his ass. So I gotta do a lil' more digging. You know how that shit go?"

"Yeah, well, we gotta be careful. Since Roberto ain't no longer in the picture, Emilio done took full control of Humboldt Park, at least with the Kings. Dem Latinos over there ain't gon' play no games about homeboy either, so if ever we move in on him, we gotta go hard. Shit, the first thing we gotta do is to make sure that he even had anything to do with Sodi getting killed. Once we figure out that mystery then we can move on to something else bloodier with that fool." He took three tokes off the blunt. "In the meantime, I got some shit I need you to help me with. You finna be surprised as hell, my nigga, but just remember that it's that season. It's time to eat like a starving fat bitch."

"What you got up your sleeve, Juelz?"

"Nigga, don't even worry about it for now. Just chillax, and roll wit' a nigga for a minute. We headed out North."

***

About thirty minutes later, Juelz pulled his Benz into an apartment complex right off of Howard. As we were pulling into the lot, about ten lil' young niggas ran in our direction with hand pistols in their palms. I grabbed the Tech .9 from under the seat, and cocked that bitch, ready to get to spraying. "Yo, Juelz, why you acting like you don't see all them lil' young niggas running up on us right now?" I questioned and rolled down my window so I could get a few good shots. I was aiming for heads. Fuck the bullshit.

Juelz grabbed my arm. "Nigga, chill. These lil' niggas wit' me. They on security right now." He pulled the Benz into the lot and grabbed a .45 from the center console of the whip, sliding it under his shirt. "Come on, let me introduce you to the fellas."

I didn't know what this nigga was on, and I for damn sure didn't trust Chicago's northside niggas. Most of them were from the Robert Taylor Home Projects, and the Cabrini Green Projects. Once the city closed both Housing Projects down, the residents flocked all over the northside, but that was after they had already been raised to be shysty cutthroats. I knew Chicago like the back of my hand. All of the hood niggas that were born here were born and raised to be cutthroat killas. Plotting, and scheming by any and every means. So, I kept that Tech on my side because I felt it was necessary. I had way to many enemies to do anything less than that.

I stepped out of the car and looked around the big parking lot. There were cars parked all over it, but there were also a lot of open parking spaces. The apartment complexes that we stood in back of looked rundown, and were spray painted with graffiti. Five point stars decorated the buildings. Juelz stood in front of about twenty lil' young killas. Most of them were wearing hoodies with red bandanas covering half of their faces. He shook up with them and gave them half hugs.

I stepped closer into their lil' meet and greet. Majority of the young dudes there mugged me with hatred. I clutched the Tech more firmly now. I was getting the wrong vibe off of these young niggas and I didn't like it. They had their guns out, and so did I. Any false move and I was going to finger fuck my Tech like it was prom night and I was in the backseat with a bad bitch.

Juelz came over to me and slid his arm around my neck. "Y'all see this mafucka right here? This is TJ. This my mafuckin' brother. This da only nigga in this world that I'd kill and die for. This my Nub." In Chicago, when one of yo homeboys called you his

Nub, that usually meant that he would die for you with no hesitation. I didn't know why we used the phrase Nub, but we did, and have been for years.

The young dudes continued to look me over. Then slowly but surely began to give me nods in the *whut up* fashion. That eased my tension just a little bit. I still kept my hand in the Tech, and was ready to spray they ass.

"Yo, TJ, these lil' niggas hustle for us. Most of them are from our old stomping grounds of the Cabrini Green Projects. They done heard about how we get down in these streets. The ones that aren't from the Greens are from right around this area. They just wanna get rich, and buss their guns for us until they get rich. The loyalty is here. Trust me on that. All my killas are battle-tested and approved." He assured me. "Come on, let's gon' into the building now." He kept his arm around my neck while we walked into the building.

I checked over my shoulder a few times, and marveled in the way that the young killas spread out and went right back on security as if they had been trained well. I eased from under Juelz's arm. I didn't like being that close to no nigga. Not even him. "Bruh, when you put all of this it together?" I asked peeking over our shoulders again.

"What? You thought I was just sitting on my ass while you were in the Bing?" In Chicago the word Bing was often used in place of the words jail or prison.

"N'all, nigga. I ain't know what you was up to. But tell me what I'm about to walk into right now."

"Nigga, Heroin Heaven. You finna see." He smiled and continued to lead the way. When we got close to the entrance of the door, two young killas stood up from the bushes with red ski masks, and Assault Rifles in their hands. Juelz held up a hand. "Yo, it's good. This my nigga right here." He assured them. They nodded, and sank back into their posts. He smiled at me again. "This shit coming together."

We entered into the glass door of the apartment building. As soon as we walked through I smelled a strong stench of coke being cooked. The aroma was enough to give me a serious headache. It reminded me of the Projects that Juelz and I grew up in. There were two armed guards in the hallway with assault rifles in their hands. They nodded to Juelz, and looked me over, before looking back out of the door on security. The further we moved into the building the more armed young men I saw.

When we got to the hallway there were two armed young killas walking up and down the hallway with black ski masks on their faces. They nodded to Juelz as well, and brushed past us doing their rounds.

We stepped onto the third floor, and I noticed that all of the doors to each apartment were opened with the aroma of crack cocaine being cooked coming from them. Juelz led me inside one of them. As soon as we walked through the door there were two armed guards on security. They looked to be no older than sixteen. In the living room was a long table where there were eight people seated. On the right side the dudes were chopping up the crack and weighing it on a scale. As soon as it was weighed they slid it across the table where it was placed into mini green Ziploc bags. I knew from just eyeing the work that they were bagging up dimes. The ones that were chopping the Yayo were breaking off of two kilos that were present. To my right in the kitchen were two butt naked dark skinned females with masks over their faces. They were chefing the dope like pros. Thick clouds of smoke entered into the rest of the apartment. I covered my face.

"Nigga, it took me a hundred thousand to get this part of the operation going. A hundred gees, and now I'm seeing three times that shit weekly. With the exception of what I gotta pay back to Jay and his people. This is eating, my nigga. Come on."

I kept looking around. The two dark skinned bitches in the kitchen were strapped. Their titties bounced on their chest while they went over around from one big pot to the next. Inside of the kitchen was a lil' young dude who appeared to be about fifteen. He had a shotgun in his hand watching their every move. Juelz walked over to him and whispered something in his ear. He nodded, and Juelz walked off. Then the young solider gave me a *whut up* nod. I returned it.

"Aiight, TJ, this next spot is where that real cheese coming in at. This the shit I'm finna need your help with because I don't trust nobody other than you." He said as we climbed a flight.

As soon as he opened the door, I had to pinch my nose. It smelled like straight funk. I'm talking ass, must, dirty pussy, and shit. The hallway had the lights turned off, and there were killas walking up down the hallway with red beams on the tips of their guns already activated. In addition to them were a bunch of heroin addicts laying along the wall of the hallway. There was just enough light for me to make them out. They groaned as they stuck the syringes in their veins and moaned as the poison was pushed into their system. The few females that I saw were shirtless. They licked their dry lips and closed their eyes as they allowed for their highs to take over them.

We stepped inside of one of the other apartments where there were twelve dope addicts butt naked, shooting up their dope. They were seated on the carpeted floor. There were two naked females that served them their dope with masks covering their faces. Behind those females were two armed bodyguards. The light in the apartment was red. It felt gloomy inside. The smell was ridiculous.

A butt naked red bone female with a nice body walked up to Juelz with a mask covering her face. She lowered it. "Huh, Daddy. This twelve thousand right here. This is just from this morning." She batted her eye lashes at him.

Juelz took the money and stuffed it into two of his pockets. He grabbed her to him and kissed her on the forehead. "Good job, Shorty. You keep handling yo business and you gon' get the tuition that I promised you."

She nodded and covered her face back. "I'ma hit you when it get to that amount again." She walked off with her ass jiggling. I couldn't take my eyes off of it. Juelz peeped me. "Nigga, that's a Project Bitch. She seventeen and working for her college tuition. I love this shit. I see you checking that ass out. You wanna fuck somethin'? I can arrange it?" He asked seriously.

I shook my head but kept staring at her. "You said you needed my help. It seem to me like you got everything under control. "

Juelz shook his head. "N'all, homie. I got shit popping in Indiana too. It's way too much for me to oversee on my own. Plus, you already know how Chicago is. Anytime a nigga doing it like this, it's gon' be a gang of niggas that wanna knock me off of this pedestal."

"So, what you saying?"

"I'm saying we gotta take a good look at a few rivals. Knock them niggas off, and then I wanna give you this building for you to oversee. You could make every bit of fifty gees a week. I already got the law on the payroll."

I kept looking around. Running a whole building full of killas and addicts was definitely something I could do. That dope boy shit was already deeply embedded within me. "Nigga, what's the catch?"

"Ain't no catch. We split shit down the middle, and we eat together. Oh, and whenever I gotta holler at the higher ups down south, you gotta roll out that way wit' me. That's all. What you think?"

"Nigga, for fifty gees a week I'm on it. Introduce me to everybody, including the police that you got on deck. I wanna make sure that I know what is what."

"Bet those. Let's start with this floor. I'm finna introduce you to everybody, and then we gon' go back downstairs and work our way outside to the hittas out that way, and then Twelve."

We did just that. Juelz made sure that everybody working under him knew who I was, and how things were going to be ran. He spoke with a killa and authoritative way about himself. Over the next week my position would be reiterated to our troops over and over, until we were sure that they got it.

"Aiight, TJ." Juelz said eight days later. "I'm pretty sure that everybody understands what it is. Now it's time that we holler at these hating ass niggas around the corner." He slammed a hundred round clip into his Mach .90, and puffed on his blunt at the same time. "You ready?"

I grunted and slid a clip into my assault rifle. "Nigga, do you even have to ask?"

Chapter 8

Later that night, Juelz scooted closer to me, and rolled his ski mask down his face. "You my nigga, TJ. You should already know that, but I wanna say it anyway. You're my mafuckin' nigga. Let's waste as many of these mafuckas as we can. They finna be out here deep as hell having their lil' meeting. We finna break all that shit up."

I positioned myself in front of the sliding door of the Chevy Astro Van. Assault Rifle in hand. This was going to be my first time bussing an AR .33, and I was a lil' nervous because I'd heard that them mafuckas be kicking a lot. I didn't want that to affect my aim. Juelz had already told me that the opposition deck only had about sixty niggas. I had a hundred-round drum. I figured that if I could hit fifty, and he could hit about fifty, then we could clear their ass out, and move into that territory instead of worrying about when they were gonna come for us. I wanted to get this shit done and over with. "Yo, you trust Kid that's driving? How old is he?"

Juelz nodded. "That's my lil' homie. He thirteen, but he know how to handle that wheel. Trust me on this." He tapped the back of our driver's seat.

The lil' boy looked back at him and gave him a thumbs up. Then he slid a mask down his face. I noticed that the van had been peeled up along the collar. Peeled up meant that it had been stolen by use of a screwdriver.

There were three other shooters inside of the van as well. They were masked, and also equipped with assault rifles. Juelz supplied them with the old school AK47, after receiving a shipment of them from Jay. We called their rifles Bin Ladens in Chicago because he had made the use of AK47s famous to use in our city. Their clips held fifty shots.

It was seven o'clock at night. The sun was just starting to go down. My heart was pounding in my chest. I knew I was about to take more than a few lives, and even though most niggas made it seem like that shit was easy, I wasn't one of them. Anytime you killed a person, their spirit tormented you for a at least a week straight. It was longer than that if you actually knew the person. The spirit of my lil' brother JD was still haunting me nightly. I often woke up in cold sweats with the sheets stuck to me. So, killing a ma'fucka wasn't as easy as the movies made it seem. There was a price that came with it. As soon as you took a life, you knew from that point on that yours would be taken in a similar way. It was like your angel that had once been protecting you abandoned you, and his post was replaced by the Angel of Death.

Our young driver made a left. He drove down the next block, and took it to the corner, until he made another left. Once he made this left he slowed down just a bit. According to Juelz our rivals were supposed to be having their get together at the park right off of Howard. It was connected to the neighborhood's Boys and Girls Club. This worried me because I didn't wanna accidentally hit up no innocent ass kids. Juelz didn't give a fuck, but I knew how my conscience worked. An accident like that would have mentally killed me. There was no way I felt like being haunted by some little kids' spirit, especially if it was a little girl. A little boy would fuck me up too, but there is something about harming a little girl that would crush me.

As we got close to the park, our driver slowed the van. "Yo, big homie, I'm starting to see ma'fuckas right now. What you wanna do? Y'all wanna get out right here, or we on some Compton type shit?" He asked.

Juelz raised up to look out of the windshield. "N'all, we ain't finna get out right here. Make a round so I can see what the business is."

"Will do." He looked over to the shooter in the passenger's seat. "Nigga, watch my sides. Anythang look funny, you pop that ma'fuckin' cannon. You hear me?"

The Shooter in the passenger's seat didn't look a day over twelve. He nodded and held the shotgun at the ready. His face looked determined. "I got you, Shorty."

As the van came up on the park I peeked out. I saw that there were two groups of dudes posted in lines as if they were in some sort of military formation. They rocked all black fits. Even their boots were black. In front of them were a few other niggas that were talking as if they were giving them orders. "Yo, what the fuck these niggas on?" I asked Juelz.

"Bruh, I don't know. In a minute they finna be on the ground though." He tensed up. "Aiight, lil' homie, circle around this bitch, and then when you get about this far next time stop, so we can open his doors and get to popping they ass up. Ain't no ma'fucka finna fuck up my operations."

"I got you, Peep." He pulled off and got ready to follow Juelz's commands.

I continued to scan the park. I saw a lot of dudes, and only a few females. They looked like they had a few cats that were on security. Real basic, and nothing that worried me. Behind the place where they were grouped up were the basketball courts. They were full of young kids from the hood balling. For a second I worried about my bullets travelling that far, and hitting one of them, but I shook that shit off. I didn't want to get to overthinking shit. We had a mission to complete, and that was that. Sodi crossed my brain, and I got to reminiscing about some of the things that we had done together. I was wishing that I had treated her better our last few times together. Before those thoughts could take over me, we had already circled back around, and it was time to handle our business. As our driver was pulling up, the Boys and Girls Club school bus pulled up right in front of the park, and the kids started to run off of the bus, and toward the entrance to the Boys and Girls.

"Awright, let's handle this business." Juelz said. He reached for the handle to the sliding door.

Our driver pulled up as close to the crowds as he could get and brought the van to a halt. "Handle that ma'fuckin' business!" He said, turning around to look at us.

The passenger lowered his window and stuck his shotgun out of it. Juelz slid the side door all the way back. I saw kids running toward the entrance. It looked like it was every bit of sixty of them. I started to panic.

Juelz hopped from the van and got to spraying. "Bitch ass niggas! Gang-gang!" *Boom! Boom! Boom! Boom!*

There was so much screaming that I felt like I could hear each individual person that was doing it. I jumped out beside him, aiming purposely for our oppositions. *Boom! Boom! Boom! Boom!* The assault rifle spit rapidly in my hands, popping out shell after shell. I washed one man out after the next. Large holes filled their backs and knocked chunks out of their faces and necks. Juelz stood beside me looking through his scope. Whacking anything moving. Then he took off running toward the enemy as they tried to flee in the opposite direction under heavy fire.

I kept popping. Running up on ma'fuckas that were curled up on the ground, finishing them with no mercy. Before I could properly identify how they looked I kept it moving. It was harder for a spirit to haunt me if I didn't know how the person looked that it came from, as crazy as that may sound. It was the truth. For me, there had always been an art, and rules to whacking a ma'fucka. My assault rifle continued to spit, until it clicked in my hand that it was empty. I could smell the burning of the steel, and gun powder. It made my nose itch. My ears were ringing like crazy, and the shooting had brought upon a pounding ass headache. Yet my adrenalin was still going. I ran back to the van and pulled a .45 off of hip. "Nigga, bring yo ass on!" I hollered to Juelz.

He kept popping, backing up, making his way toward the van. When he was about thirty yards away some nigga came from under the picnic table with a .38 in his hand, and his arm around little girl's neck. He aimed, and fired three rounds at Juelz. Juelz didn't even flinch. He got to bucking back at him. His bullets ripped the left side of the little girl's face off. The man flung her to the ground and took off running.

Juelz tried to buss but his gun clicked empty. "Fuck!"

I jumped out of the van and took off running behind that nigga. Because of him there was a little girl dead, caught in the crossfire. I was on his ass. When I got close enough I bussed the .45 back to back. One of the bullets slammed into the back of his head, and made it explode. He kept running for five paces before he fell face-first to the grass. I stood over him, and popped him two more times, before jogging back to the van. On the way I stepped over the little girl that Juelz smoked. She didn't look a day over eight. Dark skinned, her hair freshly done up in pink and white barrettes and balls. I shook my head and jumped into the van. Our driver skirted away from the curb.

***

"Nigga, that's how you handle that business." Juelz said, thirty minutes later while we were in the basement of his Trap house right off of Sheraton. "We pulled up, we handled our business, and we got the fuck up out of there. That's teamwork, baby." He placed his hand on my shoulder as he stood over me.

"Nigga you fanned down a lil' girl." In Chicago, whenever a nigga say that you fanned something down it just meant that you gunned it down on some killa shit.

"What?" He asked, turning a bottle of Rosé up.

"I said you killed a little girl. A pretty lil' sistah too. Shorty couldn't have been no older than eight."

He took his hand off of me and shrugged. "Shit happens, nigga. My aim ain't perfect. It's that nigga fault more than mine. He ain't have no right putting her lil' ass in my line of fire." He took another sip. "That's why you sitting in this ma'fucka looking all crazy and shit. Man, fuck that lil' bitch. She wasn't yo daughter." His eyes looked wild.

I stood up and stepped into his face. "Nigga, you sound stupid as fuck. You changed over a kid. A fucking baby. It's awright for you to have a little remorse over that." I said getting vexed.

"Well I don't, nigga. Like I said, fuck that lil' bitch. Shit happens. This is Chicago. Shorties get killed all the mafuckin' time. This bitch is a warzone. It been like that since the beginning. Don't take that shit out on me. At the end of the day, dude put her lil' ass in my way; I just handled my business. Bitch should've been in the house."

Before I could stop myself, I punched his ass so hard that the bottle of Rosé went flying across the basements. It shattered on the floor against a trunk full of fully automatic weapons. "Watch yo ma'fuckin' mouth, nigga. You gettin' beside yo self. She was a baby. Fuck wrong wit' you?"

Juelz had fallen to one knee. He held his jaw looking up at me. He slowly came to his feet. He stepped into my face. "Nigga, I owe you one for saving my life in Jamaica. That's the only reason I ain't finna get at yo chin right now. However, you done used that pass up. If you ever put yo hands on me again, we gon' fight until the death. That's on my mother." He looked me in the eyes as he said these things.

"Nigga, if you ever talk like you been talking in front of me again then I'ma have to test that theory. Ain't no hoes over here. You my nigga. When you wrong I'ma check yo ass. I expect you to do the same to me."

He kept mugging me. Slowly but surely his mug softened, and he smiled at me. "You always been tender over the bitches, nigga. I wonder why that is." He pulled me in and hugged me.

Our driver came into the basement along with the passenger, and the other two shooters that were in our van. "Man, you called us, big homie?" The driver asked.

"Yeah, y'all come here." Juelz ordered. He waved them over.

They came and stood before him. All four looked up to Juelz with honor. I could tell that they were waiting on him to praise them for a job well done. But this was Chicago. They must've lost sight of that.

"Y'all handled y'all business. That was real gee shit out there. Y'all seen the news?"

The driver nodded. All four of them were facing away from me. "Yeah, that shit all over the news. They making it seem like it was some kind of terrorist attack. My mother said..."

I took a deep breath, and felt my heart go heavy as I upped my .45 and stepped behind the driver and domed him twice. I side-stepped and took out the passenger next. The other two took off but Juelz was able to finish them before they got to the steps. In Chicago, you couldn't trust niggas to keep your secrets. You had to be smart. What me and Juelz did this night was necessary. That didn't mean that their spirits didn't start to attack me right away, but it came along with the territory.

T.J. Edwards

Chapter 9

After we pretty much annihilated those rivals around the corner, our hustle game took off like a rocket. Juelz backed all the way up and gave me the apartment building on Howard Street, and I got that bitch to rocking hard. He introduced me to a plug that delivered China White at eighty-five percent a brick, which in Chicago was a steal. Most of the work coming through the Windy City had been stepped on so many times that it was basically trash. But not this plug. His name was Kammron, and he was one of those heavy hitters out of Harlem, New York. Every time he came down to Chicago he was in something foreign. On the first day I met him, me and Juelz were sitting in front of Popeye's Chicken right on the corner of Howard when Kammron pulled up in a cherry red Bugatti. He stepped out of the car dressed in a Gucci suit with four gold chains around his neck, and plenty rings on his fingers. He was about five feet ten inches tall. Caramel skinned, with deep ocean waves. In the backseat of his Bugatti were two big ass security guards. Both were well-armed. But the way I had shit set up, if I wanted to chop that nigga down I could've had him, and his two Shooters chopped to pieces with one wave of my hand.

Juelz walked up to him, and they hugged. "What it do, fool?"

"Ain't nothing, Son. Yo, I was rolling through, and I just wanted to see the face of ya' right hand man. This Kid right here?" He asked Juelz.

I was fitted in a black and red Supreme fit. The tips of my dreads were red, and I had my TJ piece flooded with bloody-colored diamonds. I nodded what's up to him. I didn't know if I liked New York niggas or not. I felt that they thought they were harder than us down in Chicago, and that all we were in Chicago were gang bangers. That shit was so far from the truth.

Kammron stepped up and gave me a half of hug. He threw me for a loop when he cuffed the back of my head. I almost pushed his ass off of me. "Yo, nice to meet you, Kid. You fucking wit' Juelz the long way?" He looked me over closely.

I looked across the street and saw the poles of three of my shooters leaning out of the apartment windows with their rifles in their hands. Across the street, two more were peeking from the gangway, watching my every move. Two bitches that were inside of Popeye's looked at us from over their shoulders. Both were armed with hand pistols in their purses and ready to kill on my command. I smiled. "Yeah, this my nigga right here."

Kammron continued to look into my eyes. "Yeah, well guess what, TJ?"

"What's that, homie?" I felt on edge. I didn't like this nigga's demeanor. He seemed way too cocky to be in the heart of my slums.

"Nigga, I'm finna make you a rich ass nigga. You looking at a real live Coke King. Harlem bred. We just caught a stupid plug on the dog food, and you niggas down here in the Chi are going to be the first to get it.

We gon' turn this bitch out. Word is bond." He hugged me again and gripped the back of my head.

A month later, and me and Juelz flooded the Northside of Chicago with that life shit coming out of Harlem. Kammron made sure he had packages sent down to us every Wednesday and Friday. And we sent his money straight through the US Postal Service. Had that shit priority tracked and certified mail. Kammron said it was the smartest and efficient way to move, and I had to agree with him. All it would've took was for one dirty Postal Service worker to open up a few of the boxes that we mailed out to Harlem and they would've been set for a long time. Lucky for us nothing like that ever happened.

I got to see so much money that it spooked me. The same building that Punkin had given me to fix up and rent out, I took it and housed all of my dope boys and girls. Gave them the apartments and took the rent out of their weekly pay. Most of them were hustling just to be able to have a place to stay at night, so that shit worked out in my favor. I'd charge them half of what I would've charged a regular tenant, and put a sack in their hand, after giving them the knowledge of what I expected back in return.

I had three apartments that I used as straight safe houses. Kept two armed security guards in each one at all times. Then there were other apartments that I used as cook houses, and others as bagging up posts. I had a smooth operation going. The success of it had me more nervous than when things were going bad in my life.

***

Punkin gave birth to our son on May 4th. He came into the world weighing six pounds and seven ounces. He had a head full of curly hair and deep dimples that I was sure I passed down to him. I waited for the nurses to clean him up a little bit before they placed him into my arms. I sat in a chair beside Punkin while I looked him over.

She eased up on her elbows. "I don't know how you did it, TJ, but that boy look just like you. All he got from me is my nose." She appeared weak, and out of breath. She reached over and ran her fingers over his curls. "What are we going to name him?"

I didn't know. I still couldn't believe that I was holding a pure form of me. I had so many murders under my belt that I was already afraid for my son. "Baby, I don't know. All I do know is that I gotta protect him with my life. Damn. I love him already."

Punkin smiled. "Boy. You're supposed too. He's your first born child. Come on, I'll give you the honors to give him his first name."

I held him up in the air with the blue blanket wrapped around him. His eyes were closed. He was sleeping. I could see his eyelids fluttering. He favored my mother. I even saw hints of Marie in him. "Yo, this gotta be my junior right here. He's my first born. The purest version of me." I held him back close to my heart.

"Long as you promise to be in his life as much as you can, then we can name him exactly that." She reached up, and pulled me down so that our lips were touching.

I kissed her, and seconds later I was tonguing her ass down. My right hand, the one that wasn't holding the baby, even pinched her nipple. Milk squirted out of it. She flushed in embarrassment but that shit even turned me on.

She pulled back. "Baby, are we going to try to raise him together?"

I looked at my son again. How could I not try my best to make things work out with his mother for his sake? He deserved at least that. "Yeah, I'm wit' that. First, we gon' do what we gotta do for him. Then we gon' work on being together for each other. How that sound to you?"

She nodded. "I'll go for that. We have to take things slow and go from there." She snuggled back into her bed. "You gon' be here for a few minutes or you got somewhere to be?" She closed her eyes.

"Why you asking me that?" I held my son like a football. Leaned down and kissed him on the forehead.

"Oh, because I'm tired from pushing him out. I need to rest for a minute. That's all." She smacked her lips, and slowly opened her eyes. "What? You think I was being smart or somethin'?"

I carried my son to his crib beside the bed, and slowly placed him inside of it. "N'all, I was just wondering why you would ask me something like that. Say, Punkin, I appreciate you for giving me a healthy baby. It means the world to me." I settled beside her bed and took a hold of her hand.

"Prove it." Her voice was hoarse.

I grabbed a juice box from the counter beside us, and stuck a straw inside of it. "What you mean by that?" I placed the straw to her lips so she could wet her whistle.

She took a short sip, and swallowed it. Adjusted herself on the bed again before sitting up. "I think we should raise this baby together for real. I think we should be responsible, and that you should leave those streets alone. I don't wanna see nothing happen to you. Especially not now. Me and your son need you."

"Damn, why you gotta wish that bad luck on me like that?" were the only words I could come up with. I knew that she had a point. There was no way I could be in those streets and be the kind of father that my son deserved for me to be. But I was already addicted to the life. I was addicted to the fortune. The drama. And the power that came along with me calling for the portion of the northside of Chicago I did.

"Boy, ain't nobody wishing bad luck on you. I'm just saying that there has to be another alternative for you other than the streets. We need you now. It is no longer just about you. If ever you needed a reason to stop doing what you're doing, all you gotta do is go over there and look at your son. He is your reflection."

I paced on the side of her bed. My chains clanking into each other were the only sounds heard in the room with the exception of the machine monitoring her blood pressure and vitals. "Yo, I'm getting that major money now, Punkin. I ain't gon' be doing this shit forever, but for right now I gotta get this bread. Ma'fuckas depending on me to make shit happen."

She sat up even further. "TJ, we depending on you. Besides, I ain't hurting. I got enough money to float us for a minute. I can help you invest into something legit. You can go back to school. What about your books? Maybe we could focus, and put some of our time and energy into them?"

"Fifty gees a week." I snapped.

"What?" She looked confused.

"That's the minimum of what I'm making, doing my thing out there. Out of that fifty gees I gotta take care of my lil' niggas and the hoes that run under me. Just because I had a baby don't mean that I stop being their bread winner. It don't mean that their situations change. So, n'all, fuck that. I just can't up and stop. I'm too invested."

She shook her head. "You think those niggas out there really give a fuck about you? Huh? You think that if you got killed tomorrow that they wouldn't find somebody to take your slot and to do the same shit that you're doing? Huh?"

I saw that her blood pressure was rising on the monitor. It started to spike real fast. "Yo, chill ya' ass out. It ain't that serious."

"N'all, you don't tell me to chill out. You need to open your eyes and put your big boy pants on. Dem streets ain't gon' get you nothing but killed."

Even though she was right I felt like she was attacking me. I got irritated quick. "Yo, so you think

I'm just finna become some homebody type nigga, working a nine to five? Living paycheck to paycheck, or even worst by living off of my woman?"

"I ain't say all that. You could do your own thing, but you could do it the right way. What's the matter with that?"

"Because I'm in too muthafuckin' deep; that's what's wrong with it. I got ma'fuckas trying to take me out the game every day. They don't give a fuck that I got a new son. If they catch me slipping, they gon' blow my shit back."

"All the more reason you need to leave them streets alone and do it the right way." She said calmly.

I shook my head and stopped in front of her. "You knew I was a street nigga before you gave me the pussy. You let me bust that ma'fucka open, and skeet all in it. You should've known that no baby wasn't gon' change me. I'ma provide for my seed with that dope boy money. I'ma make sure that he got everything he need with these Trap blue faces. That's the way that shit gon' work. This is what I got to offer."

"We can't use that."

"What?"

She exhaled and ran her fingers through her unkempt hair. She looked tired and worn out. "If you aren't going to give us the best that you got then we don't wanna be a part of you at all. I will raise our son on my own."

I frowned and cringed at the same time. "Bitch, you finna start this shit with my seed on day one? Really?"

"I think you need to leave, TJ, before I have them call security up in here. You're obviously not in the right state of mind."

I rushed the bed and grabbed a handful of her hospital gown. Balled it into my fist. "Bitch, if you ever try and keep my son away from me, I'll stank yo ass. Word to Jehovah. You hear me?"

She looked into my eyes and lowered hers. "TJ, if you don't let me go, you're going to regret it. I don't know what you think this is, but I ain't afraid of you, and I ain't Sodi. Get yo muthafuckin' hands off of me!" She screamed. Her loud pitch woke up our son. He started to screaming at the top of his lungs.

Juelz stuck his head in the door. "Congratulations, ma'fuckas." He stepped in the room and tried to hand Punkin a bouquet of red roses.

She mugged him and picked up my son. "Juelz, take him out of here. He getting on my damn nerves."

I stood there heated. "Yo, Punkin, why you on this bullshit?"

"I ain't on nothing, TJ. You are not ready to be a father. When you are, you'll know where to find me. Bye."

I was so mad that I felt like popping her ass. I hated her guts in that moment. "So, you gon' shit on me because I'm in the streets? This how you feel?" I asked as calmly as I could.

"N'all, I'm shitting on you because I already see how you're going to shit on your son if I allow for you to be a part of his life. It's best that I cut that off right now. We can do better without you."

"You-You hear this bitch, Juelz?" I asked, shaking in fury. "I should murk this bitch, right?"

"Yo, TJ, she just wilding, bruh. Give her a few days to gather herself. She could be going through that postpartum depression shit. They say that always happen to women after they have kids." Juelz said this resting his hand on my shoulder.

"I ain't got no postpartum depression. I'm thinking logically for the safety and wellbeing of my son. And since I am thinking like that, it's best that TJ removes himself from the equation."

I felt like I was about to explode. I made a move toward her, and Juelz blocked my path. "Come on, bruh, think about what you finna do."

I froze in place, feeling murderous. Then I swiped his hand away from me. I looked down at Punkin, and directly into her eyes. "Yo, I know you feeling some type of way because of my lifestyle. But that's my seed. He got my blood running through his veins. He need me just as much as he needs you. I don't give a fuck how you feeling right now; you need to get over it because I am going to be a part of his life one way or the other."

Our son had been screaming the whole time. Punkin pulled back her gown and helped him to latch on to her left nipple. This quieted him. His screaming was replaced by suckling noises. She looked up to me.

"You can be a part of his life when you decide that he is most important. Until then, you need to act like he doesn't exist."

As she these said these words I lost it. I pushed Juelz to the side and made a move for her. He grabbed me around the waist. Her nipple popped out of our son's mouth. He started to scream. Two nurses opened the door and came into the room. I stopped in my tracks. Vexed. I mugged Punkin and eased out of her space. Taking one last glance at my Junior on the way out of the door. I didn't give a fuck what she was talking about, I was going to be a part of his life. I didn't care what I had to.

T.J. Edwards

Chapter 10

"Aiight now, TJ, I know you been going through some thangs with yo baby mother and all that. Running the Northside got you all stressed, and you look like you done aged five years. But it's all good. Juelz to the muthafuckin' rescue." Juelz said, holding a bottle of Moët in his right hand. He stopped and took a long swallow from it, then wiped his mouth with the back of his hand.

"Yo, what you got planned for me, Shorty? You got a mafucka down here at two in the morning and shit. I'm tired, and I just wanna get some sleep. I got two major shipments coming tomorrow, and I wanna be on point for them."

Juelz waved me off. "Nigga, bump all that. We finna do the damn thang on our Chiraq shit. You know how the game go down here. Once a ma'fucka get to having that major money, we get the first fruits of everything in the hood, including bitches. Walk with me." Juelz stepped up to his two-story townhouse and nodded at his security that were standing in the shadows of his porch, and there was another one in the bushes. Before he even turned the key in the lock I could hear the music coming from inside. He pushed in the door and stepped to the side so I could walk into it.

The lights were dimmed, but my eyes zoomed into what was present right away with no problem. The first thing I noticed was the smell of perfume, and marijuana smoke mixed. Somehow the perfume resonated more to me than the bud smoke did. The second thing that grabbed my attention were the amount of bad bitches dancing in lingerie in the middle of Juelz's living room floor. They were slow grooving and popping their asses to the Cardi B track coming out of his speakers that were hoisted up in each corner of his living room.

"Nigga, these bitches straight from the Projects. Young, bad, and probably ain't even had no dick yet. Matter fact, I know they didn't. That was the criteria. I'm 'bout to start a whole new revolution with these lil' bitches." He whispered to me. He locked the door behind us. "Have fun, nigga, take a load off." He laughed.

Before I could slip my light jacket off, two thick ass red bones slid over to me. Both were about five feet three inches tall, with long curly hair. They were strapped. Every bit of a hundred and forty pounds or better. Sexy. The slightly darker one had green eyes. I didn't know if they were fake or not and I didn't care. She rubbed her small hands over my chest and stepped on her tippy toes. "Hey, Daddy, are you the one that Juelz been telling us about?" She asked with her lip gloss shimmering.

Her friend ran her hand over my pants' front. She found my piece quickly and cuffed it. "Damn, I see you come packing." She fell to her knees and unzipped me.

I took the .40 Glock out of the small of my back and handed it to Juelz. He cuffed it. "Bruh, y'all can use that room right upstairs. The first door on your right." He strolled off into the crowd of women and placed his arm around two of them.

I pulled the second girl up from the floor and led them upstairs. Once inside I closed the door, and I locked it. "Yo, how old is you hoes?" I asked needing to make sure that they were grown. Females in Chicago grew up fast. You'd be thinking that you was fucking with a grown ass woman just by the looks of them until they opened their mouths.

The darker of the two smiled. "You ain't gotta worry about all that, Shorty. We from the 'Jects. We know how this shit go. Niggas our age ain't got shit that we want." She opened her satin robe and revealed a flawless body. Her breasts were at least a double D. Her pussy was fat and shaved clean. She ran her fingers through her slit, then sucked the digits into her mouth. "Mmm, you finna want some of this young pussy. Trust me on that. I'm tired of waiting.

Her friend squeezed my dick tighter. She pulled my pants down. I stepped out of them. She took my pipe and stroked it with her eyes wide open. "Damn, Lacey, this nigga got plenty meat. He finna fuck us over."

Lacey slid her middle finger into herself. "Bitch, speak for yourself. I'm ready for all that. Tonya, gon' head and suck it for him so we can see how big it really get." She stepped over to me, and kissed my lips, while Tonya slid my piece into her mouth as far as it could go. Her mouth felt hot, and wet. Her lips were tight. Sucking slow at first. She pumped me with her right hand, while her face went back and forth faster and faster.

I tongued Lacey's ass down. My fingers slipped into her crease. She placed a foot up on the big bed to give me better access. Now I was really finger fucking that cat at full speed.

She closed her eyes, and held the headboard with one hand, and my shoulder with the other. Her hips got to bucking forward over and over. "Mmm. Mmm. Mmm. Shoot. Damn. Unn. He finger fucking the shit out of me." She moaned.

Tonya popped my dick out and looked it over. She kissed the head and looked up at me. "We ain't never fucked nobody before, TJ. Juelz said you gotta be our first."

I stopped kissing Lacey for a second. "Bitch, y'all get down like this? Some ma'fucka done definitely hit these pussies before."

Lacey shook her head. "Un. Unh. I swear to God they ain't. You gon' be able to tell when you get in there, too. If we lying, you can tell Juelz and he already promised to throw us in the river." She said. "But I ain't worried about that. I know I'm a virgin, and so is Tonya. All we ever did was suck on something and play with each other." She ran her tongue over her lips, looking down at Tonya.

"Shorty, I don't care about none of that shit. Tonya, you keep handling yo business down there while I get her right up here."

Tonya licked around the head, and slid me back into her mouth, following the same motions as before.

That shit was feeling so good that I could feel my heart thumping in my chest.

Lacey sucked on my neck, and bit into me with her teeth. "Let me know when you ready to hit this coochie. I'm ready to give it to you right now." She growled. We got to tonguing all over again.

I gripped a handful of Tonya's hair, and fucked her face slowly. Lacey broke our embraces and laid back on the bed. She scooted back until her back was against the headboard. Then she opened her thighs wide. Her pretty pussy summoned me.

I pulled out of Tonya's mouth. She made a loud suction noise and looked up at me confused. I crawled across the bed. My dick dragging over the covers until my face was between Lacey's thick thighs. I sucked her right pussy lip into my mouth, and tugged on it, before doing her left the same way. Before she could react I had her clit trapped, flicking my tongue from left to right at full speed. Then I was sucking on it like a nipple. She bucked forward and arched her back, screaming. Her nails went into my dreads. She humped into my face, squeezing her left breast. The nipple stood out from her areola every bit of an inch.

Tonya came and stood on her knees beside us. She rubbed her meaty pussy, watching me pleasure her friend. Then she leaned forward, and they began to lick and suck all over each other's lips. Smacking, and breathing heavily. Tonya would jerk on her fingers when their kissing became too intense. I strained my neck watching them, and eating Lacey's pussy while they did their thing. The scene made me harder and harder.

Tonya fell to her stomach. She reached under me and took a hold of my piece. I turned on my side, still eating away. She stroked it at full speed. "I wanna go first, TJ. Please. I wanna go before she go." She laid on her side and backed up into my lap. Took a hold of me again, and ran my dick head up and down her slit. Her heat was welcoming.

I jumped forward and buried two inches into her gap. She tensed.

"Szzz, wait." She held me without moving.

I took my face away from Lacey's pussy. She groaned in disappointment. She kept rubbing her clit furiously until she came, screaming at the top of her lungs, bucking on the bed. "Fuck. Fuck. Fuck. You gotta fuck me now."

I took a hold of Tonya's little hips and pulled her back into my lap, forcing her to take more than half of me. She hollered and grabbed a handful of the bedsheets. Balled them into her fist. I got to pounding that fresh pussy like a savage. She was a lil' Project bitch. It was my duty to fuck her like an animal for her first time. It was something like a rite of passage.

Bam. Bam. Bam. Bam.

I rocked that cat. Digging my fingers into her sides. Her pussy was as tight as a closed fist. It kept trying to squeeze me out, but I wasn't going. She was as wet as a Jacuzzi, and just as hot. Her fat ass booty crashed into my lap over and over again. The scent of her sex was driving me crazy.

Lacey stuck her face between our bodies and licked all around down there, with her fingers between her own thighs, searching, and fingering. I slapped her ass, played in between her cheek. My middle finger dipped into her rosebud a quick twenty times. That drove her crazy. She came again and flipped onto her back still playing with her gap.

Tonya got on all fours. She laid her face sideways on the bed and gave that ass up to me. I gripped that waist and started fucking her so hard that I was damn near out of breath by the time I came, skeeting in that pussy. I pulled out and bussed all over her jiggling ass cheeks. Squirt after squirt. Her pussy's gates were wide open, leaking our fluids. She fell forward on her stomach, breathing hard, jerking every so often.

Lacey grabbed my dick and sucked all of the fluids off of him while she looked me in the eyes. Then she popped me out and laid on her back. She placed her feet on the bed, bussing her pussy wide open for my sights. I fell between those thick thighs, and slid in. Found her barrier on the inside like I had her friend's and bussed through that ma'fucka with one hard lunge forward. I sank deep into her lower belly. She arched her back. Sweat glistened on her forehead. Her eyes were shut tight. I placed her right knee on my shoulder and fucked her as hard as I could on my Chiraq shit.

"Uh! Uh! Shit! Wait! Oooo-a!" She growled.

My hips were a blur. That pussy felt better and better with each thrust. I caught myself making noises deep within my throat because it was so good. I watched my dick go in and out of her. Her lips would open wide when I pulled back, then seem to disappear when I slammed forward. She was dripping so bad that there was a puddle under her ass. That motivated me.

"I'm cumming! I'm cumming! Aww fuck! This grown nigga killing this pussy! Shit!" She screamed. Then got to shaking like she was having a seizure.

Tonya stuffed her face between our sexes now. She licked up what she could, before her and Lacey got to making out like they were in heat. Her big ass was in the air, jiggling while she leaned down and kissed all over her friend. I slid two fingers into her box and kept right on fucking Lacey until I pulled out and bussed all over her stomach and titties. It was like I couldn't stop cumming. As soon as it came out, Tonya licked it up hungrily. She humped back on my digits.

Afterwards we would collapse on the big bed. Each one of us breathing hard.

"TJ, you 'bout to let us be down with your team? We can be loyal to you. Ain't no way you finna kick us to the curb after you done did all of that." Lacey said, rubbing all over Tonya's ass as Tonya laid her head on Lacey's breast, nursing on her right nipple.

"Yo, I'ma holler at Juelz and see what he got planned for y'all. If he willing to give y'all up then y'all can come and fuck with me out North and be Gang-Gang out that way. Sound good?"

Both girls nodded in unison.

Chapter 11

"Yo, you ain't never been out to New York before, TJ. You finna love this shit. After we buss this move for Kammron he gon' take us on a tour of Harlem. That's where he from. Dem niggas out there get that stupid cash, Shorty; trust me when I tell you dis." Juelz said as we pulled into the city of New York. It was eighty degrees outside. The sun was shining bright, and instead of us rolling with the air-conditioning up, we had the windows rolled down, taking in the fresh air of the city.

"Nigga, I don't give a fuck about what they doing out there in Harlem. We Chicago niggas. We gotta make sure that our city is eating. That's the only thang I care about." I snapped. I had a bit of a headache. I didn't know what was wrong with me, but I had been catching them a lot lately.

"You looking at shit all wrong. I don't give a fuck how much they eating out this way either, but since we plugged with Kammron, that shit matters. Long as bro eating out here by the semi-truck loads, we gon' be eating down in the Land." In Chicago, us locals sometimes referred to it as the Land. We only did this when we were far away from home, or out of the city. For me, Chicago was my homeland. It was my birthplace, and the city that turned me into a radical, blue-face money getting monster.

"Yeah, well next time you should lead with that. Why you say this nigga want us out here for anyway?" I needed to know. I sparked my blunt again and got to taking that bitch to the head. I as blowing on that Purple Haze. It might've been throwback, but it had me right where I needed to be.

"He want us to pull up on a few of his rivals. I guess he got some potential threats trying to invade Harlem. We need to blindside them, whack they ass, and the homie gon' send us back with a big bag for doing it." Juelz punched in an address on his GPS system, waiting the proper directions to pull up.

"Yo, we already checking big bags back in the Land. Ma'fuckas ain't gotta be thirsty to make that gwop no more. We damn near hood rich." I puffed on my blunt some more. I got to thinking about Punkin. It had been a few weeks since I'd seen lil' TJ, and I was missing him like crazy. I was actually missing her ass too. I didn't know why I was, but I was.

"Unfortunately, the underworld know how I got into the position that I am in. Shit, that we are in. I can't just up and shit that murder for hire shit now. If I did then it's a big possibility that the Mob would send a mafucka to get rid of me. They would consider me turning my back on the roots of my success. In the Cartel world that is punishable by death."

I shook my head. "Damn, nigga. So, you mean it don't matter how successful we become in this game in our own right, them mafuckas gon' always wanna come and try to bully us around because they helped get you started while I was on lock?"

Juelz nodded. "Precisely. That's just the way the game go. For as long as we in this shit, we owe them favors. The higher we climb, the more they will use us when the time is right for them. Ma'fuckas think that once you starting to see those major chips that all of your problems go away. But that ain't the case. The more money you see, the worst shit get for you. It's always been that way. It's fucked up, but it's the truth."

"Then what the fuck are we doing?" I asked. What Juelz was saying was starting to fuck with my brain. I didn't like feeling trapped, and everything that he was explaining sounded just like a trap to me. We sounded like another nigga's bitch. I wasn't with that.

"What do you mean, TJ?"

"Nigga, I'm saying we out there pounding the pavement every single day, trying to get it while the getting is good for ourselves and our lil' ones. Ma'fuckas been going hard too. But what is the use of constantly moving up the ladder if the end result is the Cartel coming to whack us, and take everything away as soon as we wanna do our own thing and branch away from them?"

Juelz shrugged. "Nigga, I don't know. I'm only nineteen. I just wanna ball and stay wit' that drip. Splashing. Fuck the Cartel. If they want us to hit up some shit every now and then for them, then so be it. It really ain't no big deal. At least to me it ain't. We been killing shit since before we really knew how to hustle. That killa shit is in us. Ain't nothing we can do about that."

I sat back and got inside of my own head. I had a son. I had to do right by him. I had to give him a better life than what my father gave me. My plans were to run checks all the way up, and then step out of the game deathly. Once I got that bag right I was going to invest in my books and movies. That's what I ultimately wanted to do.

"Nigga, why you get so quiet?" He took the blunt from me.

"Bruh, how do you view life?"

"What you mean?"

"I mean, what do you want out of this ma'fucka? What are your hopes and dreams? What do you see for your future?"

He snickered. "Nigga, all I wanna do is ball. I wanna have so much ma'fuckin' money that a nigga can't tell me nothing. I'm already starting to get plugs all over the country. The more plugs, the more money. I wanna be a legend. I'm talking Al Capone. Sam Giancana. Flukie Stokes, or like that nigga King. Those were all legends. We gon' be the ones from Chicago. You can bet that."

"So, all you see is this hood shit. You don't wanna do nothing else?"

"Nope. I ain't finish school, nigga. Fuck you want from me?" He mugged me. "I'm from Chicago, land of the killas. I'm a murder, and a Dope Boy until the death of me. Anything else, or any other profession ain't for me. It's as simple as that. You see, TJ, I know what I am, and where I'm going in life. The sooner you realize that you ain't gon' be nothing more than the same thing that I am, the sooner you'll be able to embrace that shit and be the best at it."

I kept my comments to myself and escaped to the recesses of my mind. Was he right though? Was I nothing more than a murder and a dope boy with a hunger for bad bitches, and fly ass foreign whips? I didn't know. But we were doing shit with no effort. I went from being a stick up kid, to a young nigga of nineteen with fifteen city blocks in one of the deadliest cities of the United States of America. That said a lot. And even though I felt like an accomplished street savage, I knew that there was more to me than just the slums. "Yo, Juelz, I'm finna start writing again."

"Writing what?" He asked irritated.

"My books. That's somethin' that I can fall back on. I know how to paint a picture of this life that we live better than any other nigga in the game that just be flexing like they lived this life. Nigga, don't you understand that I'm nineteen, and I got more than twenty bodies under my belt already?"

"Shit, I got more than fifty. That mean, I can write too?" He joked.

"Nigga, I'm fa real. I wanna be able to make movies about this shit. I want ma'fuckas to see what we saw first-hand so they can understand our struggles."

"Yo, you get to putting too much shit on paper a ma'fucka might have to knock yo head off. If they don't, the feds will." I could tell he was serious.

"That's why that shit gotta be written under the guise of fiction. They can't hold fiction against you in the court of law. And as far as a ma'fucka knocking my head off about what I put on paper, I ain't gotta worry about that because I know how to write in such a way."

"Nigga, how much money you think you can make doing that?" He asked, looking at me as if I was a damn fool.

"Don't know. I guess when the time is right I'ma find out."

"Yeah, well, if you get to making some millions then I'll fuck wit' you. Until then, fuck them books. I fuck with kilos, and create dead bodies. Chicago or nothing. Fuck the world if it ain't the Windy City. I'm a trapping killa. It is what it is."

I understood where he was coming from. And even though he had a right to feel how he was feeling, I refused to except that I was nothing more than the dope game and murder game. I had to do better for my seed. I didn't know how to make the transition, but I was sure that I knew somebody who did.

***

Kammron stayed in a seedy part of Harlem right off of a Hundred and Fortieth and St. Nicholas. Just looking around his hood reminded me so much of Chicago that I got to getting homesick. Just like we had a bunch of ran down abandoned buildings, so did they. They had a lot of apartments that had been closed down with green boards smacked on the front of the windows. That usually meant that either the city had condemned the property, or that the feds ran through that bitch with a vengeance.

I saw a lot of vacant fields. Corner stores, and dope addicts roaming around like they were on their last legs. I could tell they were addicts because I was a trap star. I could spot a fiend from a mile away. The way they hugged themselves when their bodies were ached for their next fix. How they danced from one foot to the other unable to be still. The state of their unkempt appearances. Their demeanors that always seemed to be on to the next hustle of play. Just like Chicago was frivolous for these sort of addicts, Harlem was also ridden with them.

"Yo, I just wanted to take you lil' niggas through the heart of my city. This is the set right here, nah mean. My stomping grounds since I was yay-high." Kammron said, looking over his shoulder at me.

There were so many long lines of dope addicts waiting to be served around a few of the apartment buildings that I was sure that it wasn't hard for the law to make out what was taking place. I mean I was from a distant land and it wasn't hard for me to make out what was going on. Much of the area of Harlem was just like this.

"I make a million a day out here right now, Dunn. That's a million in cash. On check day it's more than that. I love my hood. I can't live in this mafucka no more, but it's all love. Word up."

"That's how I feel about the Land, Shorty. Chicago is my life." Juelz added. He looked around the slums of Harlem with a smile on his face.

"Yeah, it's good here though. Got a few clowns that just moved down from Yonkers that's trying to fuck all that up though. You already know the Kid can't have that. That's why I'm calling in my Chiraq niggas. Blindside these bitches, and go home with a hundred thousand apiece, and a new plug on some shit coming out of Vietnam that's ninety-five percent. My word the quality hold up too." Kammron smiled. "What you think about that?"

"That shit sound good to me. Real good, actually." Juelz looked back to me. "What you think, TJ?"

I was missing home and my son. Harlem looked much too like Chicago for me. "Yo, you already know I'm 'bout what you 'bout. Kammron, what's the danger factor?"

"These niggas real cocky, Dunn. Niggas don't think they can be got, so the risk level is minimal. I'ma have you niggas take care of this light work at a drop-off. They supposed to be getting a shipment of coke from my mans Jimmy tomorrow night out in Newark, Jersey. You niggas gon' make the drop-off, and whack these niggas. They never send more than two. It's a nigga named Jada, and another named P. Smoke them bitches, and that's gon' be that. Y'all keep what's in the trunk, and I'll add the chips later. Feel me?" He smiled. His neck was flooded with all different color diamonds. He rocked a pair of Gucci shades. He had chunky rings on each finger. His drip was fucking shit to say the least. I envied that nigga for a few minutes. Had I still been on that stick up kid shit I would have slumped him, took every thang, including the McLaren we were rolling in.

"Yo, this shit is as good as done. Set it up with ya' mans, and we gon' make it happen." I said.

***

That night, I was feeling so sick from missing my son that I hit up Punkin. She answered on the eighth ring. "What's good, TJ?"

"How is Junior?" I asked, settling into the hotel bed, kicking my Jordan's off.

"He's well. And so am I, in case you were wondering."

"I was. I apologize for not asking you that first. I just really miss him."

"It's okay. When are you free? Would you want to come and see him tonight?" She asked. I could hear Junior in the background making baby noises.

"N'all, not tonight. I need a few days. Can we arrange somethin'?" I was anxious. I scrolled through the pictures on my phone of my son as I spoke with her.

"I'll be going out of town this Friday for a week. If you can get here before then I would be okay with you seeing him."

"Out of town? Where the fuck you going?"

She took a deep breath. "That is none of your concern. That's my offer. Will you be able to make it over here by Thursday?"

"I'ma do my best. Yo, you ain't been having no niggas around my seed have you?"

"Goodbye, TJ. Hopefully, I'll see you Thursday." She ended the call.

I felt like I had been gut-punched. I wanted to snap out. I felt my temperature rising. My chest got tight. My vision was so blurry that I needed to close my eyes. I lay there with the worst migraine I had felt in a long time. I missed my son. I needed to find a way to get as much custody of him that she had. I hated going days on end without seeing him. I stretched out completely in the hotel bed with so many negative thoughts going through my head that I was thankful when I finally fell asleep.

Chapter 12

"This gotta be the easiest two hundred thousand that you done made in your life. Ain't it?" Juelz asked sitting in the passenger's seat of the black Acura.

I glanced into my rearview mirror, and saw Kammron still giving orders to the two females that were loading the trunk up with the dope that we were supposed to drop off to Jada and P. The car shook from them packing it into the trunk nice and tight. "Yo, we only getting a hundred a piece. That's first of all. Secondly, we don't know how these niggas get down out there in Yonkers. What happens if they get on some fuck shit just because they never seen us before?"

The trunk slammed. I glanced back into my rearview mirror again. Kammron was giving some light skinned nigga with long braids a hug. He walked away from him and headed over to Juelz's window. Juelz rolled it down.

"Yo, Dunn, it's all there. Y'all good to go. Remember to put two in each of their faces. Make sure them niggas are dead, not just twisted. Nah mean? Worst thing we can have right now is either one of them ma'fuckas laying up in a hospital bed. A dead man can't tell no tales. Ya' feel me?"

Juelz nodded. "Yo, this ain't our first Rodeo, Cowboy. We got this. You just have that cash ready. You feel me?"

Kammron laughed. "Yo, that's good. I'll fuck you in a minute, Slim."

"Say, Kammron, let me ask you a question, homie." I needed to figure some shit out because a few things weren't making sense to me. When things didn't make sense to me it was impossible for my brain to focus in on anything else other than what I couldn't figure out.

He stopped in his tracks and stepped around to my side. Behind him were two Latin broads with half of their faces covered by red Gucci bandanas. "What's good, Son?"

"Yo, you said that nigga Jimmy was ya' mans right?" I asked, looking him over carefully.

"Yeah, that was Jimmy that just bounced up out of here. Why what's good?"

"Yo, if he trapping weight like this, why the fuck would it be okay for us to knock off one of his customers? Especially if they copping chickens this heavy?"

Kammron laughed. He looked past me to Juelz. "Yo, this is New York, Kid. We do shit way different out here." He scratched his goatee. "Not that I gotta explain myself a nothing, but these niggas are more problems than they are beneficial. Out here, if a mafucka look like they getting close to stepping on your toes, you eliminate the problem before it grows muscle. You feel me?"

I nodded. "Yo, but what ya' mans gon' have to say 'bout all dis? Ain't that gon' cause a conflict between you and him?"

Kammron shrugged. "I'm a king. Jimmy fall under me. I got Harlem, and I know what's best for Harlem.

Now y'all gon' 'head and handle that business and get on back. Time is money." He smiled and tapped the hood of the car.

I pulled off. I didn't have a clear-cut understanding as to what was taking place out there in New York, and I guess it wasn't my place to. I just felt like it was best for us to handle our business and get the fuck up out of there.

"Yo, you always gotta rattle a cage, Shorty. Damn." Juelz snapped. He let down his window and stuck his elbow on the sill of it.

I came off of Seventh Avenue and got on to Interstate 95 headed to New Jersey. "Fuck wrong wit' you?"

"You, nigga. You know how this game go. The more questions you ask, the more it make niggas suspicious of you. Who gives a fuck what him and Jimmy got going on? Nigga, that ain't yo business. Jimmy ain't hitting our hands wit' shit. Kammron is. Fuck Jimmy." Juelz growled as he ran his fingers through his Mohawk and shook his head.

"Yo, I don't give a fuck what you talking about, Shorty. We all the way out here in New York. I don't know how niggas get down out here so I gotta use my Chicago logic. If you my nigga, and you got a customer that's copping chickens by the bundles, why the fuck would I off him? That a put a dent in yo pockets. Then when a ma'fucka ask me why I'm doing what I'm doing, I pretty much say fuck you. That I run Chicago, and that you run under me? Nigga it sound like him and Jimmy got some sort of animosity against one another."

"Once again, fuck Jimmy. That nigga ain't putting no bread in our pockets. If he and Kammron beefing then hopefully Kammron a hit our hand to knock his head off next. I'd be with that shit. Murder is murder if you ask me."

I laughed. "Nigga, where you think you going when you die?"

"To Killa's Heaven. Ain't no way God gon' hold how I am against me when he made me this way. How fair would that be?" He eased back into his seat, and pulled a fat blunt out of his inside coat pocket.

"Dawg, you ain't finna spark that."

He looked at me like I was crazy. "You got me fucked up. Why ain't I?"

The Interstate was moving at a nice pace. Cars zoomed past us. I flipped it on the cruise control, and kept it at an even sixty-eight miles an hour. I wasn't trying to have the State Troopers pull me over for shit. "Because, nigga, if one of them ma'fuckin' police get close enough to us they gon' be able to smell that Ganja coming out of the window. Even worse than that, let's say these ma'fuckas pull us over and they wanna run a dog all around the car? It don't matter how good Kammron packed that shit up back there if it's weed smoke all over the car."

"Dawg, you be panicking. All that shit ain't finna happen. Besides, weed is legal anyway." He grabbed his lighter and flicked it.

I yanked it out of his hand. "In Illinois. Not in New York."

"Nigga, it's legal in the whole United States. Where he fuck you been at? Now give me my lighter."

I exhaled loud as fuck. "Juelz, that shit is state by state, bruh? That shit ain't legal out here. Of you don't believe me then Google that shit. If you right, I'll give you your lighter back."

"You gon' give me my ma'fuckin' lighter anyway, but we'll play your game first." He grabbed his phone, and I guessed he Googled the question. He read the answer and mugged me. "Nigga, fuck you."

I laughed. "Yeah, nigga, I know."

He tucked the blunt back inside of his jacket. "That's why Chicago is the greatest place on earth to be."

"I agree. Now let me ask you something." I switched lanes and pulled in front of a beat-up pick-up truck that had dark clouds of smoke coming from the muffler.

"What's up?" He got to fucking with the music and settled on a track by Tee Grizzley.

"You ever think our heads will get so big in the game that we wind up turning on each other?"

"Hell n'all. Were brothers, TJ. We done been all we had for a long time now. I could never turn my back on you for any amount of money. You the only ma'fucka I love in this world."

"That's how I feel too. I'll never turn on you, dawg, under no circumstances. That's my word."

He smiled. "I already know. Now let's go and handle this business."

***

If I thought that Harlem looked grimy, it didn't have shit on Newark. Newark looked rundown. It looked like it was the place that niggas and bitches from Harlem and Chicago went to die. The roads were bumpy. The air was stale. There were projects everywhere. I saw more than skinny prostitutes that looked like they were dying. There were groups of dudes on every street almost. They looked like they were waiting for some shit to pop off. Every red light that we stopped at it appeared to be somebody selling colognes or trying to wash the windshield of the car. I was on edge like a ma'fucka.

"Shorty, we gotta get the fuck up out of this city quick. This ma'fucka look dead." Juelz said, looking around.

Jada and P arranged for us to meet them at a barbershop on the eastside of town. We were supposed to park directly in front of the shop right at nine o'clock when it closed. I waited until 9:05 before I pulled up and cut the engine.

There was a heavy-set dude waiting in front of the shop. He had a black hoodie covering his head, with both hands inside of his jacket. Juelz peeped him first. "Nigga, you see buddy ass laying up against the shop right there?"

I did. I was strapped with two Desert Eagles. I was on point. If push came to shove I was prepared to gun his ass down. Before I could even throw the car in park the nigga from the wall made his way over to our whip.

"Yo, you finna blow this nigga, or you want me to?" Juelz asked, sliding his Glock from under his coat.

"Wait a second. Let's see what his bitch ass do." I advised.

"Awright, but I'm letting you know I'm knocking big chunks out his shit if we get to blowing."

The nigga knocked on the window. Then he took a step back and let us see his hands.

I rolled down Juelz's window. "Yo, what up, Kid?" I hollered.

"This P, Dunn. Jada sent me out here to meet you niggas." He looked back toward the barbershop.

Juelz opened his door and slid out. The next thing I knew he was shaking up with him, and they were laughing. Juelz looked back to me and gave me the eyes of death. They seemed blank, and cold. They were his murder eyes. I had seen them so many times before. I was sure that I had my own pair.

When I got out of the car, P led us inside of the shop. The curtains were already drawn, blocking us from seeing anyone from outside. Inside were two other dudes. One of them appeared to be about the age of sixty or better. He had a gray beard, and a barber's apron around his body. The other was slightly muscular and fitted in diamonds. He wore a Yankees fitted cap to match his Timb's.

"Yo, this my mans Jada right here. He been expecting you boys."

Jada extended his hand to me. "Jimmy running a lil' late ain't he?" He said with a froggy voice. "I told you niggas to be here ten minutes ago."

"Yo, traffic was a bitch. That's my bad. But let me get this straight. You're Jada and he's P, right?"

Jada frowned. "Yeah, homie. Why is that important?"

"Aw, I just wanted to make sure." I upped both Desert Eagles and got to blowing them bitches back to back. I watched my first six bullets smack big pieces of meat from Jada's face. He flew backward and landed hard. I turned to P and popped him four times through the neck. He twisted in the air and fell over one of the barber chairs before sinking to the floor in a puddle of blood.

"Please, young man. Please. I don't know what they did. But it ain't got nothing to do with me. They were just here for a—"

Juelz slammed his pistol to the old man's cheek and knocked his tongue out the back of his head. He dropped the floor. Juelz stood over him and dumped three more facial rounds into him. Then did the same to both Jada and P before we bounced from there, and out of New Jersey.

***

Early the next morning we met up with Kammron at his mansion out in the Hamptons. Kammron busted up laughing as he sat on the couch. He slapped his thighs and threw his head back. "Damn, you lil' niggas didn't waste no time, did you?" He fit the last of the two hundred thousand dollars into the duffel bag and zipped it up.

"Hell n'all, we didn't. Like you said, time is money." I grabbed the bag and held it at my side. "And we ain't got time to be playing no fuckin' games."

Kammron stood up. "You know what, TJ? Nigga, I like you. That's a good thing. Always know that you got a friend in the Coke Kings. That shit y'all finna take back to Chicago finna catapult y'all to the next level. Trust me on this."

Juelz stood up. "I hope so. Mafuckas tired of fuckin' wit' these peanuts. It's time that we get to eating like we're supposed to."

"I agree. So, take this product and go hard. Step on it a few times though, or your body count is going to be ridiculous." He laughed. Then I could hear a bunch of horns blowing outside. He pulled down his blinds. "Before y'all go, I want y'all to take a gift back from the Coke Kings. I still apologize for Bonkers not being back from California, but we rolling down to the Chi as soon as he get back. Nevertheless, those trucks out there are from the Coke Kings. Enjoy." He led us outside.

When we got on there, my eyes got bucked. Outside were two newly released Bentley trucks. One of them was all black with the white leather interior. The other cherry red with the black leather interior. I rushed over to the black one. I had a habit of getting all of my shit black on black, though that cocaine interior looked good.

Juelz was already sitting in the driver's seat of the red one. He nodded. "TJ, we fuckin' wit' the Coke Kings the long way, my nigga."

Kammron walked over to me. "Remember, TJ, you got a friend out here in Harlem. Nigga, you ever need anything, you give me a call and I'ma make shit happen for you. That's my word." He gave me a half-hug and walked over to Juelz.

Juelz hugged him immediately. They got to talking. Kammron jumped inside of the truck with him and closed the door.

I ran my hand over the Bentley's steering wheel and looked around the interior. I couldn't wait to get it back to Chicago. I had plans of tricking that bitch out the right way.

Chapter 13

"I don't know how I let you talk me into this TJ, but you did. "Punkin said, three weeks after me and Juelz left Harlem. By the time I'd gotten back to Chicago she had already been gone, along with my son.

I was sick but took to grinding as hard as I could with the new product that Kammron blessed me and Juelz with. Ma'fuckas in Chicago wasn't ready for its purity. Even after a few cuts it was still as strong as a body builder on steroids.

I fixed Junior's car seat in the back of my Bentley and made sure that he was strapped in nice and tight. Then, came around and got into the driver's seat. "What you talking about, baby?"

"Aw, so I'm your baby now? Really?" Punkin looked astonished.

It was two o'clock in the afternoon on a warm summer day. The skies were clear, and it was just a bit too humid for my liking. I was worried that the heat would hurt my son. I made sure the first thing I did was turn the air conditioner on to a nice temperature before I pulled off. "You always been my baby, Punkin. I just ain't never been man enough to admit how I felt about you."

She smiled. She had a lil' gap in her teeth that made her look so sexy to me. It wasn't all that big, but noticeable. "Yeah, well you sure had a funny way of showing it." She crossed her thick thighs. Her Fendi skirt pulled back just enough to showcase her well-oiled skin. I peeped those sexy limbs and nodded in approval of her snap back. It had only been a few months but Punkin had been hitting the gym hard. Her body was already taken back its natural form. That was arousing to me. Though she still had some of the baby gut left. I thought that was sexy too. I wanted to hit that pussy, and pull our family together, and I was willing to do anything that I had to in order to make that happen.

"Well, I was immature. I'm trying to man up now and get my stuff together so I can be the man that my family needs me to be."

Now her eyes were really bucked. "Boy, I can't even believe that you talking like this. Lord, I just died and gone to heaven." She teased. She slid her Dior sunglasses onto her face and sat back after taking a peek over her shoulder at Junior. "So, where are we headed, TJ?"

"Aw, I just thought we could go down to the lakefront and have a picnic. You know, once we drop Junior off with your aunty. I think it's time that you and I get to know each other, for the better and the worst. We need to come up with a plan to make sure that we can come into existence as a family. A plan that we can both agree on, might I add."

"You might." She giggled. "Well, baby, I just wanna say that I applaud you for trying. It really does mean a lot to me. And your son. I'm speaking for him too." She looked back at him again.

"You look real good today, Punkin. I'm serious. This is probably as fine as I have ever seen you. And that's coming from a nigga that used to pull on his piece thinking about you when we were little."

"Ugh, you for real?" She blushed.

"Yep, a few times. Girl, you had that big ass booty ever since we was in the fourth grade. Then your mother acted like she couldn't see it herself because she used to always send you to school with stretch pants, and tight ass designer skirts that used to hug your every curve. It was like she couldn't help but to assist me to fantasize about what you had under them fabrics."

Punkin laughed. "Boys are just nasty. I hope our son don't be like that." She glanced back to him again.

"Yo, stop fronting. So, you mean to tell me that you were just innocent when you were little? You never touched that lil' kitty at all?"

She bit a piece of skin off of her bottom lip. "Are we really doing this right now?"

"We are." I kept rolling.

"Well, if you must know, I didn't start messing around with my stuff down there until I was about twelve. That's when my thighs got to growing, and they would rub against my coochie all the time. So, one day it was hot, and I call myself going into my friend's bathroom so I could wipe my sweaty cat. I sat on her toilet to do just that but forgot to close the bathroom door, and a big ass dog came right in and stuck his head between my legs and licked my stuff. I don't know what it was, but he gave me some weird ass sick feelings. Like he touched something down there that he wasn't supposed to have. That night, when

I went home, I stayed up to three o'clock in the morning trying to find that button that he hit. When I found it, that was a wrap. I was awakened, and it's been crazy ever since."

My dick was hard as hell. "Yo, so you saying a dog got you horny?"

"Boy, hell n'all? Are you out of your mind? Ugh. No! It was his wet ass tongue that swiped my button a few times that got me curious about myself down there. Not the animal. Let's be fa real." She rolled her eyes. Her caramel face was red as hell. "Now you got me feeling all self-conscious and shit." She placed a tuft of her hair behind her left ear.

"Baby, I was just teasing you. I know what you meant. It's all good. It's just straight to know that we both had a lil' freak in us back then. Shit, and now." I gripped her thick thigh and squeezed it. I tried to imagine her being all curious about her body back then and trying to find her clitoris. All of that shit seemed so hot to me, especially since we were in school together at that time.

"So, where did you get this Bentley truck from, and don't say you bought it either. You got yourself a rich girl out there?"

I shook my head. "N'all, this was a gift from one of my niggas from back East. He got that stupid cream, and he just wanted to extend his gratitude. That's all."

"Yeah, well he must really appreciate you then." She yawned and covered her mouth. "I hope we have a good time today. We really do have a bunch of things we need to discuss."

"I agree." I stepped on the gas and headed to the suburbs of Chicago where I would drop off Junior to Punkin's aunt's house.

**

After setting the big white blanket out on the sand for Punkin, she took the picnic basket and kneeled on the blanket with it. I grabbed two glasses and filled them with Hawaiian Punch. She took the sandwiches and placed them on paper plates. "What kind of sandwiches are these?" She asked as the water crashed into the big rocks of the beach behind her. Her hair blew in the wind, making her look all exotic to me. She appeared to be glowing. I still couldn't believe that she'd had my kid. It felt so surreal.

"Turkey, American cheese, Swiss, mayonnaise, and Dijon mustard. Why?"

"Just asking. They sound good."

"They will be."

She set up our plates, and then kneeled in front of me. We started to have our late lunch. "Well, we might as well get the tough questions right out of the way. When do you see yourself leaving the streets behind, and jumping on to something more legit?" She asked, before taking a bite of her sandwich.

"Damn, you gon' hit me there right away, huh?"

"Sure am. Go."

I looked past her shoulder and caught sight of two dark colored Spanish females. Both had on two piece bikinis that did very little to shield their bodies. I got stuck on the thongs that split their ass cheeks. Both pair were jiggling like crazy.

Punkin looked over her shoulder and followed my gaze. "Damn, boy, focus."

"Yo, I don't know when exactly I'ma step down off of my post, but I know it'll be soon. I wanna be that man that both you and my son can depend. I want for us to raise him together. I wanna be with you on some real shit, not whatever this is that we're doing." I said these words out of my mouth, but I didn't know if I really meant them. The truth was that I really liked Punkin, but I didn't know if it was enough to make me quit fuckin' wit' other hoes. There was just way too much pussy in the world for me to get stuck fucking with just one. Even though I loved Sodi, and she was probably the baddest female I had ever seen, I couldn't see myself being solely stuck on just her without no side pieces. That part of me needed to mature as a man.

"TJ, how can you say that you are ready to be with your family when you're already checking out other females while we're trying to get things together between us? That makes no logical sense. Do it?"

I lowered my head and took a bite of my sandwich. "No."

"Then when it comes to you leaving the game alone, how much longer do you honestly feel that you have out there before something seriously bad happens?" She asked taking a strand of hair out of her mouth that the wind had blew into the corner of it.

"Yo, I don't know. But I ain't done just yet. I can't just pull out and leave all of my people on the limb like that. I wish I could, but I just can't. You need to understand what is at stake for me and my people if I was to up and leave them all bogus and shit."

"Honesty, TJ, I don't care. All I care about is our family. I care about you handling your responsibilities as a man. That's my concern. And I'm sorry to say that if you cannot leave those streets alone then there is no place for you inside of our family. There just isn't. It breaks my heart to say that."

I saw the defeat in her eyes, and that terrified me. I saw her taking Junior away from me and I couldn't handle that. I couldn't lose my son. I knew I had to say whatever it would take to convince her that I would do what she wanted me to, even though I was dead set on being in the trenches with my Project Misfits. Game was game, and I had to do what I had to.

"You know what, Punkin? I love you, and I appreciate you for being a good mother to my son." I meant that part whole heartedly. "Because you are so great of a mother, and probably the best woman I could ever find, I'm gon' follow your advice, and I'ma cut the streets off, and pick up your family. I need you, and I want us to make it as more than co-parents." That was the part that I only half meant.

"Aw, baby, do you really mean that? You're going to leave the streets for me?" She dropped her sandwich and came over to wrap her arms around my neck.

I hugged her frame. My eyes found the two Latinas again. They were walking past after drinking from their bottled waters. Their side-boobs jiggling along with their asses. "Yeah, Boo. I'd do anything for you.

I mean, we are all that we have. I wanna make this work. But you gotta give me at least a month to shut everything down. That way I can let Juelz take over the operations, and I can prepare myself to start college this coming semester. Can you at least do that?" I asked in a calm, submissive voice.

"Baby, you need a whole month though? Really?" She asked kissing my neck.

"If I can shut shit down fore then I will. I'm just saying that a month will be the max amount of time that I will need. Is that cool?"

She pulled back and looked into my eyes. "Yeah, baby, that's cool. We got a deal. Wanna know how much of a deal we got?" She hugged me again with her face in my neck.

My eyes were still jocking those two Latin broads. My brain flashed to Sodi briefly. "How much?"

She stood up and reached for my hand. "I'm finna show you."

***

I sat down in the far back seat of the Bentley with my pants down. Punkin pulled up her skirt and slid her panties to the side. She held my hard dick and slid down on to it engulf me inch by inch. Her pussy felt like it was scalding me. Tyrese played through the radio. "I love you, TJ. I promise I'ma make you happy. With our family is where you deserve to be." She licked up and down my neck and started to ride me real slow. Her ass poked forward as she took as much of me as she could.

I gripped it, and bounced her up and down, humping into her box, digging as deep as I could. Within seconds we had a rhythm going. The Bentley truck moved back and forth.

"Unn. Unn. Daddy. Yes. Yes. Fuck me. Let me ride this dick." She humped faster and faster, bouncing on my shit with her mouth wide open. She looked so sexy.

I forced her to take all of me. Fucked her faster and faster, gripping that juicy ass. She had gotten a lot thicker since she had our son. That shit felt right. Her pussy snapped back as well. It felt as tight as the first day that I'd been able to get some of it.

"Unn. Unn. Fuck yeah. TJ! TJ! Uhhhh!" She hollered, and dug her nails into my side, throwing her head all the way back. She turned all the way around until her back was against my chest.

I sucked all over her neck while she rode me with blazing speed. "This that shit you been missing, huh? Tell Daddy. Unn. Unn. Tell me you. Been. Missing. This dick!" I humped up hard.

She screamed and held the side of my thigh while she bounced back on me over and over. She held the seat in front of her and growled. "I missed it. Uhhhh. Fuck! I missed it so badddddd!" She screamed and came for the third time. I could feel her walls squeezing me like a fist and vibrating uncontrollably.

I held her, steady dumping my seed into her again. Then I turned her sideways and tongued her down.

Punkin had me lost in a trance for a minute. I could actually see myself being my with her. I didn't know even then if I could be with her solely, because I knew me. But in that moment I felt as close to her as I have ever felt.

***

I laid up with her for a week straight. We fucked like crazy, all day, and all night. I felt the more that I jumped in those guts, the better the chance I had of keeping our family together. In those seven days that I spent laid up, I actually appreciated being able to wake up every morning and see her and my son together. It felt like a blessing to me. Each night before I closed my eyes I questioned if being with the two of them for the rest of my life as a family was what I really wanted. I can't say that I came to any clear-cut conclusion because the streets were calling me.

Chapter 14

"Yo, Shorty, guess what I found out, my nigga?" Juelz asked as he got into the passenger's seat of my Bentley truck with a fat ass Garcia Vega in his mouth. I could smell the Ganja.

Instead of taking his blunt out of his mouth, I sparked my own. "What's good?"

He peeked into the back of my truck and caught himself. Both Lacey and Tonya were back there with Assault Rifles on their laps, ready to kill anything that looked like a potential threat to me. They had half of their faces covered with black bandanas. "Yo, I can speak in front of them right?"

"Shorty, y'all step out the truck for a minute. Let me fuck wit' the homie."

"You want us to leave these rifles in here, Daddy, or do we bring them with us?" Tonya asked.

"Leave them bitches on the backseat. Just keep them Forty Glocks cocked and ready to go, though. You know what it is." They followed my commands, and didn't even acknowledge Juelz as he sat up front. I silently nodded at that. I hadn't had that much time with them but already my lil' hoes were trained.

As soon as they were out of the truck, Juelz turned to me. "Nigga, I found Kalvin bitch ass. That nigga fucked up. He doing heroin and all kinds of other shit. What you wanna do?"

I was so shocked by the news that I had to sit up. I couldn't breathe. Kalvin was my sperm donor. Ever since I was a child, all he'd ever done was beat my mother senseless, sexually prey on my little sister, and use me and my brothers as punching bags. Though he was my pops, I ain't have no love for that nigga. I started to imagine how my mother looked on her death bed after dude had come to the hospital and beat her up for the final time. I was vexed. Then my brain imagined his sick ass on top of my sister and I got so angry that my vision, as it did when I became angry, went blurry. I was so heated that I got to shaking. "Shorty, you saying you know where Buddy ass is right now?"

Juelz smiled. "Hell yeah, I do. That nigga holed up in one of my smoke houses on Seventy-Second and Bishop. I got my One-Way boys over there rocking up that new work that Kammron been flooding us with. Last time I saw your pops he was fucked up and laid up against the wall. I put one of the loyal Dope Head bitches on him. She twenty five, still look real good, but she been hitting that raw for a minute now. I told her to call me with his every move, and to keep on her charm until I can figure out what you wanna do with this nigga."

I started the ignition to my truck. "Yo, get out."

"What, nigga?"

"Get out so I can follow you over there. I wanna holler at this nigga like ASAP. It's time I get some answers about what happened to Marie."

"And after you get that?" Juelz leaned in with a big ass smile in his face.

"Den a ma'fucka finna perform a autopsy on his bitch ass. No mercy, and no love."

"That's the shit I'm talking about. Yo, let's switch whips though. These Bentley trucks gon' be too noticeable. I'm finna hit up the spot and have that bitch cleared out before we get there. I don't want no ma'fucka to know what we on." He nodded excitedly. "Hell yeah!" He exclaimed getting out of the truck.

All I could think about was how I was about to handle the situation. I hadn't seen my father in damn near two years. I had so much anger and animosity against him that I feared what was about to take place. But at the same time, I couldn't wait for it to happen.

***

Bomp. Bomp. Bomp. Bomp. I knocked on the door for the second time impatiently. Standing on the porch I scanned the neighborhood. It was just after nine o'clock at night. There was an odd chill to the air. It smelled as if it was going to rain. With each breath that I inhaled I could taste the salty air.

Juelz went through the backdoor of the Trap house. Minutes later he opened the front door with a smile on his face. "Yo, calm ya' ass down, nigga. I had to make sure that everything was good. I—"

Before he could finish what he was about to say I stepped inside of the Trap and nudged him aside. "Where the fuck he at, Shorty?" There was an instant smell of must and funk in the atmosphere. They had the house hot. I had only been standing inside of it for a few moments and already I felt overheated.

139

Juelz closed the door back. "He in the bedroom off the kitchen. He just getting done fucking with old girl from down the street. That bitch all skinny and shit. Yo old man done fell downhill a long way. Come on." I didn't give a fuck about all of that. I followed him to the room that my pops was doing his thing in. When we got there, Juelz stepped to the side and snickered again. I grabbed the doorknob and turned it with my left hand while I pulled the Glock out of my waistband with my right. I pushed the door inward and rushed inside.

Kalvin was just pulling up his pants. He looked over his shoulder with his eyes bucked. The dope head that he'd just slept with hopped out of the bed and ran out of the room.

Juelz snatched her up and closed the door. "Handle yo business, nigga," were his parting words.

Kalvin slid his bifocal glasses onto his nose, then put on his shirt. He looked back at me and laughed. "So, you caught me, lil' nigga. Now what the fuck you gon' do?" He pulled out a Newport Short and lit the tip of it, sitting on the bed.

I kept the gun at my side. "What happened to my sister?" I asked feeling my throat get tight.

"She dead, lil' nigga. That's what happened to her."

Now I had the gun pointed directly at him. I cocked that bitch and held it firmly. "I'ma ask you again. What the fuck happened to my sister?"

"You know why I never liked yo monkey ass, TJ? Huh? You wanna know why I used to beat you ten times worse than I beat your brothers? Do you?"

I didn't know what to say. My pops looked like shit. He was still real muscular, but his dreads had a big bald spot in the middle of them. His face looked slightly more wrinkled than the last time I remembered seeing him. Everything was gray. He smelled putrid.

"Well, nigga, I'ma tell you anyway. You were a constant reminder to me that your mother was a whore." He nodded. "Yep. Bitch cheated with her ex and brought you into this muthafuckin' world. Thought I was gon' treat you like my own son, but she had me fucked up. I ain't nobody's step daddy." He mugged me. "Marie too. That bitch didn't belong to me either."

"Yo, watch yo ma'fuckin' mouth, nigga, about how you talking about my people. Respect the dead. Word up."

"Man, fuck you, nigga. You think I give a fuck because you got a gun pulled on me? You thank I'm scared to die, Jahrome!" Jahrome was my middle name. Every time that nigga got heated at me he used it. It also happened to be his middle name as well.

"Nigga, I said what I said. " I was still taken aback. If he was saying that he wasn't my real father, then I wondered who was. It all started to make sense now. The way he treated me. How he always was all over Marie, even when she was too young to be thinking anything about sex. The way I never felt a connection to his bitch ass. How I always knew that I was going to murder him one day.

"Yeah, I got you to thinking, don't I? You thought your mother was the greatest gift to mankind, huh? You didn't know she was a THOT— ain't that what you kids call it these days?" He took a pull from his square and blew the smoke toward the ceiling.

"Yo, my mother was sixteen when she got pregnant with me. She was just a lil' girl. Anything she did, you ain't have no right holding that shit over her head as a woman. You beat her into the ground, even on her death bed. Then you took my sister from me. You ain't nothing but a coward. A bitch ass nigga in every sense of the word."

"Lil nigga, fuck you." He snarled.

"Yeah?" My heart got to beating fast.

"Yeah."

I aimed at his shoulder and bussed my gun. *Boom!* The bullet flew from the barrel, and punched a massive hole into his shoulder, knocking meat all across the wall. He jumped up and rushed me with his head down, swinging like crazy. Blood squirt from his wound.

I side-stepped him and smacked him as hard as I could with the Glock. He yelped, and flew into the dresser, making a bunch of noise. "Get yo bitch ass up, nigga. It's good to know you ain't my father. I'm finna beat you senselessly, just like you used to do my mother and my sister."

He sat on the floor with his back against the dresser for a second. Then he stood up and held up his guards.

142

"You wanna take my life, then get yo punk ass over here and take it." He spat on the floor.

I closed the distance quick. He threw a punch, I ducked it, and came back up with the handle of the gun, slamming it right into his top row of teeth.

He spat them all over the floor. Blood poured out of his lips and dripped off of his chin. "You muthafucka. I'ma kill you. I'ma kill yo ass dead." He hollered and rushed me again.

I side-stepped for the second time. Used his momentum against him to throw him into the wall. He slipped. I tossed the gun on the bed and rushed him, swinging haymakers. Connecting one blow after the next in his face. Every time I hit him, a certain part of me was healed. I could feel his bones cracking. We somehow wound up on the floor with me on top of him punching him again, and again. My knuckles smashed his face inward slowly but surely. "Who?" *Bam!* "Killed?" *Bam!* "Marie!" *Bam!* I asked with each punch.

His face caved in. His eyes were blinking, looking as if they were leaking fluids. "Deion." He hissed. "Deion." He closed his eyes.

A chill ran down my spine. I got to punching him harder and harder. Faster and faster. This was the man that raped my mother in front of me multiple times. The man that had beaten me so bad that he'd sent me to the hospital with broken bones on numerous occasions. The same man that had taken my baby sister's virginity. Then I was sure had taken part in her murder. He was a monster. The more I punched him, the harder I hit him, the more I felt like I was vindicating my mother and sister.

When Juelz came into the room and pulled me off of him, I had zoned out unbeknownst to me for every bit of five minutes fucking him up. I stood up with my hands swollen. Blood everywhere. Breathing hard. I looked down and saw that he was unrecognizable. His face was caved in. A puddle of blood formed around his neck and head. The hole in his shoulder was pouring his plasma.

Juelz smiled down at him. "Sick mafucka. That's what he get, bruh. Fuck that nigga. Don't feel no type of way."

My chest continued to heave. "I don't. Come on, let's chop his bitch ass up, and burn his remains. Fuck this nigga. I just found out he wasn't even me and Marie pops." I still couldn't believe that. I wondered why my mother never told me this fact.

"That's a good thing. If you ask me you just caught a break. Come on. I already started cutting old girl up. We can, bruh, and get rid of both of their asses tonight."

***

Later that night, after we dismembered and burned Kalvin to ashes, I couldn't help but to wonder if he had been telling the truth. I thought about all of my features and his. I was trying to see our similarities. There were few. I had always looked like my mother and not him.

Juelz hoisted the big, black plastic bag of the dope head's burnt remains on to the ledge of the overpass, and poked a hole in the bottom of it, before he busted it open. Her ashes began to spill out right into Lake Michigan. "You know what, TJ? We really gotta holler at that nigga Deion now. I knew out of the three that he was the one that had killed your sister. God don't like ugly. When we catch that nigga, we gotta make him pay."

"Yeah, I agree." I ripped a hole into Kalvin's bag, and watched his remains disperse into the air before they landed into the dark lake. The overpass was a familiar sight for me and Juelz. We had been there a few times throughout the years to get rid of bodies that we feared would report back to us. This time was no different. I felt a piece of me had been restored. I had to find Deion. I had to make him pay for what he did to Marie.

"You know what though, TJ? All dem niggas gon' meet up in hell together. I hope they burn like a ma'fucka. I know they gon' try and jump us when we get down there though. They always been cowards." He laughed and emptied his whole bag. I wondered if Juelz really understood what we had done. I wondered if he understood that I had just taken the man that I'd thought had been my father my whole life out of the game. I wondered if he honestly even cared how serious things were. But I was almost certain that he wasn't, and because he was so relaxed with everything, I became the same way.

"Oh, and before I forget. Are you still trying to get up with Emilio?" He asked, dusting his clothes off. That was one of the only bad things about the whole dump site situation. If the wind was blowing, the ashes of their burned bodies always seemed to get all over our clothes. There was no way around it.

I finished dumping Kalvin into the water. Shaking the bag to make sure that there weren't any more remnants of him. Later, me and Juelz would also have to burn the plastic as well to ensure that there was no evidence that would tie back to us. "Yeah, you already know that's a loose end. Why?"

"Just so happen that me and you gotta take a trio out to Gary, Indiana in a week so we can pick up some of that shit from Kammron."

"Wait, why are we going all the way to Gary? Why he can't send that shit right here to Chicago?"

"You already know how them Alphabet Boys get down. Ma'fuckas can't get too comfortable. Besides, it was my idea to meet up in Gary. I figured we'd kill two birds with one stone."

"What's the pickup?" I asked balling my bags up. The wind blew, and I could feel little specks of rain mixed inside of it.

"Twenty kilos. I'm keeping ten, and I was gon' send ten over there to you."

"That sound good. So, where do Emilio come into the equation?"

"That nigga got a Black bitch pregnant out that way. Yep. Supposedly it's his lil' boo thang too. I fuck wit' a few bitches that fuck with her. She told them the whole rundown, and they brought that shit back to me. Apparently that nigga love young, Black pussy. The lil' hoe he got pregnant ain't nothing but fifteen. I hear that nigga thirty."

I rubbed my chin hairs. "So, what's the odds of him slipping while he out there loafing with that bitch?"

"Nine times out of ten. She do pills, and he fuck wit' that Lean real tough. I hear he travel with two guards. Other than that, he feel secure as a ma'fucka. We can get to the bottom of that situation too. That's if you wit' it."

"I am. You say a week right?"

"At least that. I'ma get shit in order and get back at you like ASAP."

T.J. Edwards

Chapter 15

I don't know how it happened, or why I wound up showing up unannounced at Jelissa's doorstep, but two nights later the weight of my father's murder was getting to me so bad that I felt like I was being trapped. I needed an outlet. I needed somebody to talk to that I felt would understand what I was feeling and going through. I don't know why I chose to hit up Jelissa, but I did.

She opened the door with a big Bible in her hand, and a warm smile on her face. "TJ, seriously? What are you doing here?" She brushed her curls out of her face, and gave me both dimples that were prominent on her cheeks.

"Yo, I was in the neighborhood, and... Well, I guess I just need to talk. Are you busy?"

She shook her head. "No, I was just finishing up reading a lil' bit of the Word but I'm wide open now. Come on in. Take those Balenciaga's off at the door though."

I nodded and followed her inside. She had on a pleated Burberry skirt that clung to her from the waist down. It made her figure look perfect. I closed the door behind me and slipped out of my shoes. Her home smelled good. I could tell that she was cooking. "Mm! Something smell real good in here. What you cooking?"

"I'm done cooking. What you smell is my German Chocolate cake. It's patent is pending." She joked. She looked gorgeous when she smiled. She had this extra tooth in the lower row of her teeth I guessed that God put there to give her a bit of an imperfection. But to me it only enhanced her beauty.

"Well, whatever it is it smells real good. I hope you got enough for me." I wasn't really hungry, but I could eat."

"I'll tell you what, I'ma make you a whole plate. Give you some of this Jersey home cooking." She waved me to follow her. "Come on, you can wash your hands in the sink in the kitchen. It's cool."

I followed her again. My eyes never strayed from her ass. It was jiggling like a ma'fucka. "Yo, I was over in Jersey just a short minute ago, and it was messed up there. I didn't even think y'all lived that rugged out there on the east coast."

She laughed. "Boy. It's ghettoes all over the world. Lucky for me I wasn't raised in one. Yvonne didn't play that." She started to make me a plate.

"Who is Yvonne?" I got to washing my hands in the sink with her blue Dawn dishwashing liquid.

"That's my mother. She the only parent I got left. I mean, my dad is alive, but I rarely talk to him. Our past isn't the greatest. You do eat Salmon right?"

"Yeah. What else you got with it though?"

"Rice, asparagus, carrots, and that German Chocolate cake."

"Hell yeah, load me up. All that sound good."

"I bet. When was the last time you had a home cooked meal?"

"It's been a minute. Probably since my mother passed. I mean, Sodi did her thing, but it was mostly Spanish food which I grew to love."

"Yeah, but ain't nothin' like that food from a sistah, is it? Be honest. I know she looking down here, but she understand." She kept making my plate.

"You already know ain't no female got nothing on my sistahs."

"I can't tell. All of our men ain't doing nothing but kicking us to the curb so they can go and fuck with either the white girls, or the Latinas. I mean, to each their own, but damn." She gave me two big pieces of fried Salmon and set the plate before me. "You want some hot sauce?"

"Yeah."

She handed it to me, and then poured me a glass of lemonade. I felt like a boss watching her lil' fine ass move all around the kitchen making sure I was straight like she was my wife or something. I got to feeling some type of way. She made her plate and sat across from me. "So, what really brings you over this way?"

"I killed my father." I don't know why I blurted it out, but I did. As soon as the words came out of my mouth I was wishing that I never said them.

She dropped her fork. "Are you serious?"

I nodded. "Yep, and now that I have, that shit is eating at me. I can't think straight. I been having all types of nightmares. I feel like the devil is all over me worse than usual." I got to shaking when I imagined my dream from the night before of Kalvin pulling me into a lake of fire with the devil laughing at the top of his lungs.

"How did that happen? Was it an accident?"

"N'all, I fucked him up real good for what he did to my mother and sister. That nigga had it coming." I stood up. "Yo, I hope I can trust you. You told me before, that snitching shit wasn't in you. I hope you still feel the same way. Do you?"

"Your father was a monster. The things he did to your mother and Marie were heinous. I'm surprised that it took you this long." She stood up and walked over to me.

I don't know why but tears came out of my eyes. I wasn't crying for stanking Kalvin. I guess I just felt like my soul was heavy. I had so many bodies on my spirit that it was starting to weigh me down a bit. I didn't know what to do. I felt lost. I needed for somebody to understand me. I couldn't go to Juelz about the shit because growing up in Chicago you are taught as a young man that feelings don't exist. That if you show any forms of weaknesses that you were either gay or meant to be preyed on by the killas of the city. Men with emotions were considered weak. Pussies. And in the land of the heartless, dead meat or targets. I didn't wanna be labelled none of these things.

She came up and wiped my tears away with her thumbs. "TJ, it's all good. Let it out. I know that you're hurting. I know that you are in pain. Your life has been terrible since day one. It's time that you breakdown. You deserve to." She hugged me.

I unleashed all of my pinned up emotional pains. The tears fell, and they wouldn't stop coming. I held her without a sound coming from me. I thought about how my mother looked the last time I'd seen her in her hospital bed, beat up from Kalvin's hands. I thought about Marie, and how she never had a chance. I wondered if she and I even had the same father. I thought about our physical similarities. I thought about all of the people that I had smoked one way or the other. The souls that were haunting me, and the tears just fell. My heart held no remorse. I felt like it was turning colder as I stood there draining my body of its emotions.

I held Jelissa for thirty minutes straight while I released those tears. When I finally stepped back she had tears in her eyes too. I was confused. "What's the matter?" I asked looking into her beautiful face. It was my turn to wipe her tears away with my thumbs. She was so small and seemed so delicate.

She sniffled. "I know what I'm supposed to do right now in honor of Sodi. I'm just a little scared. I need to shut my thinking off, and just go for it." She exhaled and stepped up to me. Grabbed the back of my neck and kissed my lips hungrily.

It shocked the shit out of me because I could still see the Bible that she had been carrying on the kitchen counter. I picked her lil' ass up, and sat her right next to it, taking it as a sign that I was supposed to have this woman. I returned her kisses with more angst. My tongue searched and got entangled with hers.

She broke away breathing hard. "It's all good, TJ. I'm here for you." Her big nipples poked through her blouse.

I stood there looking at her for a long time. I didn't know what to do next. Her phone rang, snapping us out of the sexual zone. She hopped up off the counter and picked it up. She held up a finger, and went into the other room. My eyes followed her. I sat against the counter for a minute, and then followed her inside of the next room. She stuck a finger in one of her ears to block the noise. I couldn't hear what she was saying but it seemed like she was taking an order of some sort.

I snuck behind her and slid my hands up under her blouse. My big hands cupped her B cup breasts. Her hard nipples poked at the palms of my hands. I sucked her neck, and bit into it like a horny vampire.

She moaned and ended her call. Turned around to me and hopped up on me, wrapping her ankles around my waist. I held her up by that fat ass booty. Tonguing her down passionately. We fell to the floor of her living room. I ripped the blouse from her frame and tossed it behind me. Yanked the skirt up and tore he panties from her frame.

She moaned and opened her thighs wide. "I love Sodi, TJ. Please know that I love her. Can you say that?"

I slipped down, and pushed her knees to her chest. Her pussy popped out at me from this position. My face sunk, and wound up in her gap, eating like a trained lesbian. I had those pussy lips wide open, flicking that clit, then sucking it. Two fingers ran in

154

and out of her tight hole. Her juices seeped out in rivers. I looked up at her and kept fingering. "Cum for me, Jelissa! Cum for me. Do it for Daddy!" I went to town again.

"Uhhhh! Uhhhh! It feel so good! It feel so, so good, TJ! Shoot!" She bucked, forcing my face deeper into her gap, locking her thighs around my head.

I couldn't breathe, but I didn't care. I nipped at her Pearl until she came hard all over my assaulting tongue. I slurped her juices. She screamed and shook all over the floor. I flipped that ass over, forcing her on to all fours, slapped that ass and rubbed that juicy pussy from the back. In one stroke, I was deep inside of her womb.

She groaned, and looked back at me with her eyes in slits. "Ooo. We bogus."

I grabbed them hips and got to fucking her hard. Long stroking that box. *Bam. Bam. Bam. Bam.*

"We bogus. We bogus. We bogus. Uhhhh. TJ! Shit!" She threw her head back, and bounced back into me harder and harder. "Take this pussy then. Take it! Take it! Take it! Uhhhh! Take it from me! Shit!"

I was pounding her as hard as I could. Her gap was small. It gripped me tighter than any pussy I remembered, and that shocked me. When she laid her face on the bed and pulled her cheeks apart for me, I came hard, jerking inside of her. She felt it, and screamed. Then she was cuming just has hard. She fell on her stomach with me still long stroking that cat. Somehow we wound up with her on her side, and me on my knees thrusting while I watched my dick go in and out of her juicy brown lips. They would open to reveal her pink when I pulled back. When I plunged forward, she dug her nails into my sides and humped into me. She came.

Finally I got between her thighs and fucked her slow while we sucked all over each other's lips. She had a fat pair on her face, and they tasted good to me. I liked the way we smelled mixed together too. She had these big, pretty ass areolas that covered most of her breasts. Her nipples stood up a full inch like pencil erasers. The harder I sucked them the wetter her pussy got until we were cuming on each other over and over again.

***

In the morning, when I woke up, I found Jelissa wrapped securely in my arms with her back to my chest. My piece rested against her ass cheeks slightly inside of them. The sunlight peeked through the blinds of her bedroom warming us. Her eyes were already open. "TJ, I see why Sodi fell in love with you. Making love to you last night and most of this morning was everything that she said it was when she bragged to me about you. Damn." She shook her head.

I snuggled closer to her. Wrapped her in my big arms. Her body was so slim, but there was no denying that ass that was inside of my lap. "Yo, why do that have to be a bad thing though?"

"Because, you are not my man. You were hers. But I know what she would've done for you after you broke down in front of her. I felt like she was looking down on us expecting me to do what I did."

"Yeah, aiight den. So why you regretting it?"

"Because, once again, you are not my man." She tried to slide out of my embrace, but I kept her ass trapped. "Let me go."

"N'all, we finna get an understanding right now. I ain't trying to hear shit."

T.J. Edwards

Chapter 16

"What we need to get an understanding about?" She asked, looking over her shoulder at me.

"About us, and what we just did."

"First of all, TJ, there is no us. We connected last night, and like I said, some of this morning, but that was just fun. Now we gotta go back to our lives."

I released her. "Yo, is this because of what I told you about my old man?"

She shook her head. "N'all, it ain't got nothing to do with that." She rolled over until she was sitting up Indian style on the bed. I was able to see her pussy lips from where I sat on the edge.

"Den what is it about?" I was hoping that she wasn't about to discriminate against me because I was trapping in the streets like Punkin was. Boujee females were starting to get on my nerves. I prayed that she wasn't on that shit with me.

"It's about where I am in my life. Right now, I am too busy working on myself. I am trying to get a lot of things established, and entering into a relationship with any man just isn't in the cards for me. I'm sorry." She slid out of the bed and stood before me. She looked all athletic and sexy. Her perky breasts stood up on her chest. Her pussy was shaven clean. The lips slightly opened. She popped back on her legs, and rested with her hands on her hips. Her brown eyes were staring me down. "You feeling some type of way?"

"You mafuckin' right I am. Shorty, I ain't never said nothing about no relationship. But I do got a lil' thing for you. For some reason, when I was holding you just then, I felt complete. I ain't never felt like that when I held a female before. Not even with Sodi."

She screwed up her lips. "Boy, do you call yourself running game on me a something?"

I stood up with my dick swanging. "N'all, ain't no need for all that." I grabbed my boxers, and slid them up my muscled thighs.

"TJ, I swear I like you too. The attraction is there, but right now is not the right time for me to be getting involved with you. I'm opening another salon in two weeks. I'm still going over renovations with this restaurant on Halstead. I'm in the middle of my first novel, and I got a whole son out in New Jersey. Boy. That is a lot on my plate. I can't afford another addition. Especially not one like yo crazy ass." She smiled but I could tell that she was serious. I don't know what it was about it but the more she was trying to push me away, the more I wanted her ass. "I think we should be good friends."

I stepped up to her. "N'all, I don't wanna be your friend. I got enough of them. I need you to be more than that."

She looked up at me with her big brown eyes appearing to be stuck. "Oh, yeah?"

"Yeah." I pulled her to me. "You telling me that you didn't feel that same energy when I was holding you?"

She bit on her lower lip, and avoided my eyes. "We headed in two different directions. I keep my ear to the streets, TJ, and you out there wilding. They call you and Juelz the Hood Reapers because of y'all body counts."

"That's just talk, Shorty. I'm trying to do better for myself now. I got a son."

She wiggled out of my embrace, and turned her back to me. "That's another thing. Ain't yo son still practically newborn?"

"Yep. Why? Is that a problem?"

"Because, you should be with his mother, supporting her. Not over here trying to start something new with me." She looked disgusted.

"Me and her ain't never faked like we were going to be together. We were casual. We laid down a few times, and my son happened. We got an understanding. I make sure my son is well taken care of."

"Yeah, but taking care of a kid and being a real father takes more than money. You need to be there. I know first-hand what it feels like to have to raise a child on your own. It sucks. No female should have to go through that, and enough of our sistahs are. It's just wrong."

"You right, but I promise you, me and her got that figured out. Jelissa, I'm feeling you, and I gotta have you."

"I got me. There is no man walking this earth that can have me as if I'm merely a possession. You can be a part of me at best."

I snatched her lil' ass up, and held her up in the air. She automatically wrapped her thighs around my waist again. "Shorty, I hear what you saying, and I respect it. However, I wanna be a part of you. I can't tell you all the specifics of why because I don't know myself, but I just feel different when I'm with you. I feel like I got a heart, and I already know that mafucka been black. It been black until you came into the picture."

She held me around the neck. "Boy, you don't even know what you're saying. TJ, you're just in a weird place right now. You're lost, and you're looking for anybody that's willing to help you. Anybody that won't judge you, and that'll just go with the flow. Well, that ain't me. I might be little, but I'ma stand on yo' ass with all ten of these pedicured toes. I promise you."

"Yeah?"

"Yeah."

I fell to the bed with me between her hot thighs. Her pussy warmed my belly. "That's what I need to get me on my game. I need a strong woman that's gon' stand on me and not allow for me to get away with nothing."

"TJ, I'm not ready for a relationship. Before I build anything with you, I need to get myself in order. No man is more important than me." She rolled me over until she was straddling me. She pressed her weight down on me. Her hands forced my shoulders to the bed. "So, like I said, I think we should just be friends, and see where things take us from there." She situated her pussy so that it was over my piece. "You feel me?"

I closed my eyes. "Yeah, but let me see how you look in control though. Let me see if you can really game a nigga."

"That's what you wanna see?"

I scooted back, taking her with me. When we were in the middle of the bed, I laid back again. "What's good?"

She looked down at me for a short while before a sly smile came across her face. "Aight, we gon' do this one more time, and then we gotta give each other some space. I ain't trying to get my head all messed up like you had Sodi's." She slowly moved down my body. She stopped and looked back up at me. "Agreed?" Her hand snuck inside of my boxer hole.

My eyes rolled backward when she gripped my dick and pulled me out. "Hell yeah, agreed."

She licked her lips. "Aight den." She held me firm and sucked the head of my piece into her mouth. Sucking it slow, she focused only on the head. The sounds driving crazy.

"Damn, Jelissa. You fucking me up. That shit feel so good. Mmm."

Her tongue traveled around and around it. Then, she sucked me hard and her teeth lightly nipped at the head. This got me to shivering. I grabbed a handful of her hair.

She smacked my hand away. "Unn. Unn. Keep yo' hands out my hair. I just got my lace-front whipped." She climbed to all fours. "Huh, put those big hands on my ass. It's good." She went back to sucking and driving me up the wall.

I smacked that ass and squeezed it. My fingers navigated through her cheeks until I found her pussy. I played with the lips and humped up from the bed into her mouth. She held my hips and controlled my movements. Her head bobbed as she slurped. Her knees spread. My eyes rolled again.

She popped my dick out and looked into my face. "You shouldn't even be getting this, TJ. Only time a woman is supposed to be doing all of this is for her husband. You lucky I'm making an exception for yo' ass." She grabbed my pipe tighter, and licked up and down the pole. Then, she sucked the head back into her mouth, and went to work at full speed.

I clutched the bedsheets, whimpering. I felt like a bitch.

She squeezed me again, and nipped the head with her teeth. She sucked as hard as she could. I got to cumming hard. She beat me with her fist. My cum splashed into the air, and came back down on her fist. She sucked me into her mouth again, then cleaned up every trace of my semen like a pro. "Aight, lay back. You finna eat this pussy and then I'ma ride you until you can't handle this pussy no more." She climbed up my body, and turned around. Once her pussy was over my lips, she lowered it, and rode it slow while my tongue played over her sex. She beat my meat swiftly. "Mmm. Mmm. Yes. You getting. This pussy. For the. Uhhhh. Shoot. Unn." She rode my tongue a bit faster. "Last time. Mmm. Mmm. Mmm."

I held her hips and ate that cat like my life depended on it. My focus was on her clitoris. It was big too. Juicy. Sticking up like an erect nipple. Every time I flicked it, she jerked, and shuddered. That motivated me to keep on doing what I was doing.

"Mmm. Mmm. I'm cumming, TJ. I'm cumming. Oooo, shit!" She bucked and came hard. She squeezed my piece in her hand while pumping him faster and faster. She slid off of me, and climbed on again. Her pussy lined up, and engulfed me. She laid her face in the crux of my neck, sucking on it while she rode me slowly. Her pussy was gripping me like a glove. "Mmm. Mmm. Yeah. You feel that?"

I held her ass and made sure she was taking every inch of me. "Hell yeah. Yeah, baby. You got. That sauce." I meant that shit too. I fucked my share of women, and I had to admit that Jelissa had the best pussy I had ever had. It was tight. Hot. Wet as a muthafucka, and she could take me deep. Most other broads acted like they couldn't handle when I long-stroked their cats, but Jelissa adjusted and took that shit like a champ.

We fucked for another hour straight. Then, I fell asleep between her thighs after I came twice, and she came three times. She hugged up on me, and felt so perfect in my arms. I imagined Sodi standing over us, giving us her nod of approval before she disappeared.

***

I woke back up five hours later. Jelissa was sitting on the edge of the bed with a pink bath towel around her. "Aight. It's time to go, mister. I got some studying I gotta do before I Facetime with Rae' Jon."

I stretched, and got out of the bed. "Damn, this how you finna do me?"

She stood up, and dropped her towel. She slipped on a pair of PINK Victoria Secret underwear. Her breasts jiggled. Then, she placed on the matching lace bra. "It ain't nothing personal. I had fun. But now life gotta continue. I gotta get back on my responsible stuff. I'll hit you up when I get right. It's all good." She tossed me my pants.

I got dressed. I felt like a Flipper. Like I was about to take the walk of shame. I couldn't believe that a female was treating me like I usually did hoes. "Yeah, it's all good. I guess I'ma catch you on the rebound." I said as I stepped out on to her porch a few minutes later.

She leaned out of it and pulled me to her. She kissed my lips. "I enjoyed you, TJ. You got a lot going on between your thighs. You got me a lil' sore. I ain't gon' even lie. That's why I gotta get you out of here. The more you stick around, the more I wanna jump your bones." She kissed me again. "I'll be in touch, though. And when it comes to your lil' secret about your old man, it's safe with me. You be careful out there." She eased back into the house, and closed the door.

I felt like a straight THOT. She had straight treated my ass.

***

When I strolled into Punkin's crib later that night, she was sitting up in the living room listening to Monica on the radio, and drinking a glass of wine. She looked up at me. "Where you been at?"

"Out. What's up with you?"

She rose from the couch. "I thought you wanted to make this shit work between us?"

"I do, what are you talking about?" I didn't feel like arguing with her. I was still a little tired, and I needed to rest for a minute. On top of that, I couldn't get Jelissa off of my brain. She had just handled me like a boss bitch. That was new to me. I needed to see her ass again. I was feening for her already.

"You been out with another bitch, TJ?"

I walked into my son's nursery and looked him over. He was laying on his back in a Gucci onesie. "Suh. Damn. And nah," I lied, not wanting her to look into my eyes.

She came up beside me. "So, what you been doing for the last couple of days? Huh?"

"Punkin. I love you, and we gon' talk about this later on. I'm tired. I been trapping all night. Let me get myself together."

She nodded. "Yeah, aight, TJ. You do that. I'll holler at you when you wake up then." She eased out of the nursery, and closed the door. She stopped and opened it again. "You got passion marks all over your neck, firstly. Secondly, if you wake him up, you're spending the rest of your day trying to get him back to

sleep. I'm going out. I'll be back once I clear my head."
She closed the door.

I sighed and held my hand over where I remembered Jelissa sucking all over me. "Damn."

Chapter 17

"Dawg, why you so quiet? You ain't said shit since we hit the expressway." Juelz asked, looking over at me while he took a swallow from his grape pop. "You got something on your mind that we need to talk about?"

"Nah, I was just thinking about somebody. That's all." I continued to drive, increasing my speed to seventy. It was nine o'clock at night and rainy. And we were set to roll over to Gary, Indiana so we could hit up Emilio.

"Yo, Shorty, I know you ain't still stuck on this Jelissa broad? Fuck is wrong with you? You wilding."

"Nigga, you don't understand, and you wouldn't. That's why I don't even wanna talk about this shit right now." I kept rolling. "Turn on some music or something."

"Woooow. Nigga, are you serious right now? You finna act like this toward your brother over some pussy? Damn, that bitch got you already. Yo, I never thought I would see the day. Please tell me what's going on in your head? Seriously, I wanna know."

"Juelz, we ain't finna do this, Shorty. We gon' roll over here, and holla at that nigga Emilio. You sho his bitch got what we got planned?"

"Hell nah, but her sister is. Sheryl say that nigga be kicking the fuck out of her lil' sister, and he think he own the family all because he got Angela pregnant. She don't know what we got planned. All she thinking is that we finna come and pick his ass up. That's enough for her."

"Aiight, so what happens when we take his ass out the game then?"

Juelz shrugged. "Look, nigga, you already know how I get down. I don't give a fuck about nobody in that house, including Angela's baby. If it comes down to the point where we gotta whack his ass, then I'ma handle everybody else in the house as well. You already know that's how this shit goes."

"Yeah, well, that's cool. Fuck this nigga anyway. I can feel it in my spirit that somethin' ain't right. He had to have something to do with Roberto and Sodi getting killed. There is motive for both offenses. If he got rid of Roberto, then he became the sole caller for their troops over there in Humboldt Park. Roberto ran all of that shit before he died. Emilio was his right-hand man. If anything happened to Roberto in the rightful order, that King of Kings slot would go to Emilio, and it did."

"What about Sodi, though? What reason would he have to kill her?" Juelz asked trying to put the pieces of the puzzle together.

"Greed. Before Roberto got whacked, he gave Sodi a bunch of money and dope that he ripped off from one of the Cartels. Emilio had to know she had it. She probably didn't give it up willingly, and he took her life. Jelissa said that there was no forced entry to Sodi's place. That she opened the door for whoever came and did what they did. Emilio was like her brother. That's the only nigga I could've seen her opening the door for if I wasn't around. I mean, other than you."

"Yeah, well, it sound like all of the arrows are pointing to him. All we gotta do is get his bitch ass to confess, and then we'll know for sure. You think it'll give you closure once you find out, and we murder his ass?"

"I don't know. I hope so. I really do." I tightened my hand on the steering wheel. I saw Sodi's face inside of my mind's eye. I missed her. I wondered if I was doing the right thing.

"Yeah, Shorty just texted me a few minutes ago saying that they hitting that Tequila real hard. She sure that by the time we get over there that dude gon' be knocked the fuck out. He supposed to have two body guards with him though. They should have big guns. She didn't know what kind. They are waiting for him in the front of the house inside of a Lincoln Navigator with tinted windows."

"And she's sure that it is only two of them?" I needed to make sure.

"That's what she said. But let me hit her ass up real quick." He started texting away. "In the meantime, tell me about Jelissa, bruh. What are you seeing in this girl that's so special?"

"I don't know. I guess when I held her, I felt that weird ass electricity that them hoes be talking about in all of those chick flicks. I didn't expect to, but I did. Then she handled a mafucka real rough after we got done doing our thing. Ain't no female ever treated me like that before."

Juelz kept looking at me. "Nigga, that's it? That's all you got?" He frowned. "You tripping. We gotta take a trip to one of these islands. That's all that is. You need to be around some super bad bitches. Once that happen, you'll let this pipe dream go with these other mediocre ass hoes." He looked disgusted. "Nigga, Shorty ain't even all that, is she?" He asked.

"To me she is. I think she bad as a muthafucka."

"Nigga, you think every bitch bad. I'm saying do she got natural, long, curly hair? What's her complexion? Do she got some foreign shit in her blood, or is she just regular? I mean, come on. Give me somthin'."

"Bruh, she's a sistah. Why a female gotta have some type of mixed shit up in her before you can acknowledge that she's beautiful?"

"Because a bitch can't be beautiful unless she got some mixed shit up in her. Do you realize how many bad bitches that there are in the world? I mean, seriously?"

"Yeah, nigga. Of course, I do."

"Well, tell me how is it that you can settle for anything less than perfection?"

"Because to me perfection ain't defined by how a female looks on the outside all of the time. It's defined by her character. Her loyalty, and if she reminds me of my mother or not."

"And you saying that this Jelissa broad check all of those boxes? She remind you of your mother?"

"Yeah, she remind me of her. As far as the best of those boxes though I have yet to find those things out."

172

"Dawg, you fucked this bitch for one night, and she got you talking like a straight sucka. How the fuck is that even possible?"

"Ain't no suckas over here, nigga. I just had a good time. Shorty had me feeling some type of way. That's all."

"Yeah, she must have some good ass pussy. Maybe I should pull up on her ass in a Jag a something so I can see what that box be like between her thighs. That's the only way that I'll be able to understand what you feeling right now." He sat back in his seat, and looked out of the window. "We still taking that trip somewhere though. We gotta hit up Brazil, Puerto Rico, or Dubai. Those three places got the baddest bitches on the planet. That's how I feel."

"Yeah, well, we can do that. First, we gotta handle this business out here in Gary. Then we gotta find that nigga Deion and blow his lid back so we can close that final chapter. After that, we'll be free to live life however we see fit."

"I still can't believe how she got you feeling though. Do you know that I have never been in love in my entire life?"

"Straight up?"

"Straight up. Not even close, bruh. I done had feelings, but that shit never lasted that long for me. I was always able to shake that shit off."

"I don't know why you like that. But to each its own. I ain't in love with nobody right now either. But I'm open to it. Sooner or later I'ma have to leave this street shit behind so I can raise a family. When the time comes, I wanna know that the woman I choose I'm going to love for the rest of life. I ain't had that yet, but I felt some crazy things with Jelissa."

Juelz closed his eyes and shook his head. "Nigga, shut that shit up. Seriously. I'm willing to fight yo swollen ass if you say anything else about how you feel about old girl. Don't say that shit no more, TJ. Seriously."

"Nigga, fuck you. I like Shorty, and I'ma see what that's all about. Deal with it."

He kept his eyes closed, shaking his head. "Yeah, whatever. Let's go kill this nigga so we can get back to the Land, Shorty." He looked down at his phone. "Yo, she just hit me up and said dude trying to force her and Angela to do a threesome wit' his drunk ass. She asking me what she should do?"

"Tell that bitch to do it. To draw that shit out. Oh, and to leave the key at the backdoor a something."

Juelz texted back. "Aiight. Shit that a workout in our favor, huh?"

"Hell yeah, it will." I stepped on the gas.

***

An hour later, I sat in the driver's seat screwing a silencer onto my .40 Glock. The black ski mask already covered my face completely. "Yo, that's definitely the Navigator she was talking about, huh?" I asked Juelz.

He tied the red bandanna around the lower portion of his face. "Yep. We gotta get a move on before they done fucking. If that nigga as drunk as she making him out to be, he ain't gon' be able to last for too long." He screwed on his silencer, and tucked his .40. Both were brand new and fresh out the boxes.

"Aiight, I'ma take the driver, and you take the passenger. This street dark as a bitch so we should be good. Keep your eyes peeled though."

"Say no moe."

I opened the driver's door, and lowered myself to the street. Rain fell heavily from the sky. There was a slight wind. The constant sounds of the rain hitting the pavement resonated. I looked to my right and left to check my surroundings. The Navigator was parked a half of block in front of us. We made our way toward it hunched low to the ground like seasoned carjackers. When I go to the truck's bumper, I felt my heart pounding in my chest. I scanned the block one final time. Then rushed to the driver's window. Shattered the glass with the butt of my gun by slamming it against the corner of it. Then before I could even make out where the driver was, I was shooting.

The window crashed on the other side of the truck. I heard hollering, and I knew that Juelz was handling his business. I don't know how he got the passenger's door open, but he did. The interior light popped on. Now I could see. Both men were scrambling on the inside. Blood seeping out of them. I aimed, and fired six more rounds. Juelz fired five. The end result was both men laying limp in the middle of the truck. Their blood all over the windows, and ceiling.

Juelz closed the door back. "Come on, bruh. We gotta move." He hopped the small metal gate of the duplex and took off running down the side of the house.

I hopped it after him, and did the same. We wound up at the back door. He grabbed a key from under a big brick, and fit it into the lock, before pushing the door in. We tip toed up the back steps, and slipped into the house. I stood there for a second and sniffed the air. I smelt weed smoke mixed with cocaine. There was Spanish music playing. Every now and then I could hear the sounds of a female moaning. This made me smile under the mask. Everything seemed to be going according to how Sheryl said that it was. In Chicago you never could trust a bitch. They were more susceptible to setting you up before a nigga would. This situation was very common in my city.

Juelz tapped me on the chest. "It's murder season, nigga. Let's go."

Chapter 18

Juelz waited on the side of the bedroom door. There was a light coming out of the bathroom that illuminated a nice portion of the hallway. He held up his gloved hands, and started to count with his fingers. He held up the number one. Then two. Then three. I kicked the door inwards and rushed inside. Sheryl screamed. Angela was laying on her side getting fucked hard by Emilio. He had his eyes closed. When he heard the loud nose, his hand slid under the pillow.

Good. Juelz popped him in the back, and rushed him. Emilio fell against the pillow. The hole in his back bubbled up and spilled over. He groaned. "What the fuck?"

Angela stumbled out of the bed, and ran to a corner of the room. She wrapped her little arms around her knees. "What's happening? We don't have any money here."

A naked Sheryl ran over to hug her sister. "Shhh. This has nothin' to do with us."

Emilio groaned. "I got ten gees in my pants. Take that shit. I need to get to a hospital."

I snatched him up by wrapping my arm around his neck, and throwing him to the floor. He made a loud ass crashing sound. The front of my black hoody was drenched in his blood. My gun was aimed at him. "Nigga, why did you kill Sodi?"

"What?" His eyes got big as pool balls. "What are you talking about, Homes? I didn't kill her."

I kicked him in the chest, and held him pinned to the floor with my Jordan. "Stop lying to me. Yo homie already gave you up." I lied. Why did you kill her? Who gave you the order?"

He swallowed his spit. "I don't know what the fuck you're talking about. Sodi was like my sister, Homes. I would never hurt her. Roberto was my right hand." He groaned in pain.

I didn't believe him. I stomped him in the chest. He sounded like the wind had been knocked out of him.

He curled into a ball. "I didn't hurt Sodi. I swear to God I didn't. Me and my crew are looking for the ones that did. I swear it."

Juelz stood over him. "You paid a mafucka to rob Roberto. You said that he was supposed to have ten kilos, and fifty thousand in cash. Money that y'all ripped off from the Cartel. You gave up his mother's address, and his baby mother's. Don't you remember that?" Juelz asked.

"N'all, man. I swear. You got me mixed up with somebody else."

Juelz pulled his mask off and mugged Emilio. "Nigga, I'm the one that you hired to hit him up. Look familiar?"

Emilio's eyes looked like they were about to pop out of their sockets. "Juelz? I thought—"

"Tell my nigga why you killed his bitch."

My heart dropped into my chest. I felt like I couldn't breathe. Juelz had been a part of the equation the whole time. I wondered how I could not have known.

178

Emilio held up his hands. "Okay. Okay. Look. I swear I didn't pull the trigger. It wasn't me. I just went to go and get what Roberto had left her. That was it. She didn't wanna give it up. She fought tooth, and nail. Then when she pulled out the three-eighty, he shot her."

I was shaking so bad that my teeth were chattering. "Who shot her?" I growled.

"My lil' homie. But I took care of him already though, so you ain't even gotta worry." He assured me.

"Yo, we gotta get out of here, bruh. What are you going to do?"

Angela jumped up and ran out of the room. "Help!" She hollered.

"Angela, no!" Sheryl exclaimed. She took off behind her. Then Juelz went after them both.

I continued to stand over Emilio. "Nigga, I know you killed my lady. Yousa shysty nigga. I saw how you rotated around Roberto's funeral like you owned the place. You didn't like Sodi because of how she checked yo ass in front of me. Ain't that right?"

He frowned. "I didn't give a fuck about her. What I cared about was my money and dope. That's all I wanted. She could've gave it up with no problems, but n'all, she had to try to take matters into her own hands. She had to pull out that fuckin gun like she was tough. What was I supposed to do?"

My eyes raised. I took a step back and aimed the gun at him. "I got a message from Sodi, nigga."

"No. No. Noooooooo!" He hollered, and covered his face with his hands.

I go to finger fucking my gun back to back. Spitting bullet after bullet into his torso, arms, and face. He laid out flat. I stood over him and bussed some more. "Bitch ass nigga. Rest in peace, Mami." Then I ran out of the room.

I found Juelz in the hallway standing over a squirming Angela. She jerked naked on the carpet. Her face was filled with bullet holes. Beside her was Sheryl. She had a massive hole under her left eye with blood pouring out of it. She lay seemingly lifeless. Juelz looked over at me. "Bitches had to go. You know how shit is."

***

Me and Juelz were quiet for the first thirty minutes on the ride home. I didn't know what to say to him. I was heated and severely pissed off. I couldn't believe that he would hold such a secret from me.

When the Welcome to Illinois sign came into view, he cleared his throat. "Look, bruh, I wanted to let you know that I had offed her brother, but I just didn't know how to tell you. Then when she came up murdered, I already knew who it was from the get-go. That's why I used my resources to track his ass down, and made sure you was the one that sent him on his way. I had more than a few opportunities to do so, but I couldn't take that away from you. That would've been bogus of me."

I kept driving for another mile. My head was spinning. Had Juelz been anybody else I wound have blown his brains out all over the dashboard. I was that upset.

"Nigga, you should already know what it is when it comes to this life. I pull contracts. A mafucka drop that bread on they target and I whack they ass. I didn't even know Roberto was Sodi's brother until after the fact. That's also why I didn't go to the funeral." He looked over at me. "Damn, nigga, can you say somethin'?"

"Nigga. You killed my woman's brother, and you never told me that you did it. Second to that, you knew that this bitch ass nigga had killed her, and you waited all this time to tell me. I been going through it too. That shit hurt. You supposed to be my Day One. If I can't depend on you to keep shit one hunnit with me, then I ain't got nobody, Shorty. I ain't gon' let this shit divide us, but you got me fucked up right now. Word to Jehovah, man."

He nodded, and sat back in his seat. We rolled for another five miles in silence. Juelz kept fidgeting in his seat. "Dawg, I love you, TJ."

"I know, Shorty. I love you too."

"Yo, I'm sorry for this. Word to my moms. I ain't mean to fuck shit up like I did. You gotta forgive me though."

"I do. You my only family, nigga. Real love don't hold grudges. I got more love and respect for you than that."

He nodded. "Dawg, I owe you one. I mean that. I got you too."

***

That night when I made it back to Punkin's house, she had a nigga there that mugged me as I walked through the door. I was already feeling some type of way because he was there and I didn't know who the fuck he was. But the way he was looking at me got me super vexed. Punkin hugged me, and I kept mugging him over her shoulder as he stood in the living room with his fists balled. He was five feet seven inches tall. Stocky, with caramel skin, and long corn rows.

"Yo, who is that nigga?" I asked, ready to get on some stupid shit real quick.

She broke our embrace. "That's my cousin Reginald. He just got here from Iowa a few hours ago. He gon' be here for a few weeks until he can get on his feet."

"A few weeks? Fuck you mean? He standing up just fine if you ask me."

She laughed and slapped me on the shoulder. "Boy, you know what I mean." She grabbed my hand, and drug me into the living room. "Reggie, this is TJ. TJ, this is Reggie."

I kept mugging him. "Why you gotta lean on her, homie. Niggas down in Iowa don't know how to hustle a something?"

He snickered. "Yeah, we know how to do all of that. I just got out the feds. I'm a lil' down on my luck. It ain't gon' take me that long to bounce back."

"Yeah, I don't give a fuck what she talking about. You ain't finna bounce back in this mafucka. Pack yo shit. We finna go and get you a room."

Punkin stepped in front of me. "Baby, calm down. He's a good dude. Besides, he's on an ankle bracelet. He has to be here."

I waved her off. "Dawg, how long you think you finna be walking around this mafucka? Huh?"

"As long as I need to, homeboy. Who the fuck is you?"

"Who the fuck am I?" I pulled out my Glock and cocked that bitch. "This who I am, homie. I'll knock yo mafuckin' head off, boy. On my city!"

He threw his hands up. "Aiight. Aiight. That shit ain't that serious. I don't want no problems with you."

Punkin rushed in front of me again. "Baby, please calm down. I'ma make sure that he is out of here as soon as possible. Until then, why don't you just give me a lil' space?"

"Space? Really, bitch? What? 'Cause of this foogazy ass nigga right here?" I smacked my lips. "Man, fuck you then." I humped her ass out the way and went into my son's nursery. Picked him up, and planted kisses all over him. "I love you, Junior. Daddy a see you inna few days." He balled his little fists and yawned.

I came out of there and packed me a quick bag. Switched pistols. I left the Glock there under her mattress like I did with a few other hand pistols, and grabbed my Desert Eagles. When I made it back into the living room, Reggie was holding her, trying to calm her down. "Look, nigga. I'ma give yo ass two weeks to be up out this bitch. If you ain't gone by then, we gon' have a problem. Punkin, come here."

She slowly broke away from him and stepped over to me. "Yes?"

I kissed her lips. "Don't have that fuck nigga around my baby. I'm asking you this as a man. Can you honor that?"

"But it's his little cousin." She whimpered.

"I don't give a fuck. I don't want no nigga around my baby. Respect my mind, Shorty. Or else I can just kick this fuck nigga out." I pulled the Desert Eagle from my waistband. "You want me to do that?"

She shook her head furiously. "Okay, TJ. Please, just leave for a few days. Please. I'll get things under control here. Then, when he's out of the house, you and I need to have a serious talk."

"Yeah, whatever." I stepped into Reggie's face. "I find out you been around my baby, I'm blowing yo shit off. You understand that?"

Reggie looked into my eyes without saying a word. He clenched his jaw. Swallowed his spit, but kept right on mugging me.

"That's alright, you ain't gotta say nothing. I said my peace. Try me if you want to." I bumped that nigga and bounced. That shit with Juelz had me feeling murderous. On an average day I would have never acted the way that I did. But I was hurting, and ready to stank something. I had to hit up the slums to take my mind off of things if only for a little while.

Chapter 19

"Daddy, I'm saying, you seem like you been down the whole time we been back from the Trap. What can me and Tonya do to make you feel better?" Lacey asked stepping into my face, and rubbing her hands over my chest. Her breath smelled of Double Mint gum.

"Yeah, Daddy. We been out herr hustling a hard for you and shit. Ain't you missed us? Tonya chimed in, wrapping her arm around Lacey's lower back. She kissed my chest, then kissed Lacey on the cheek before squeezing her ass.

Lacey slid her hand into my pajama pants, gripping my dick within her fist. She tried to pump it. "I want some of you, TJ." She dropped and brought my pajamas with her.

We were on the sixteenth floor of the The W Hotel in downtown Chicago. From my vantage point inside of the room I could see a nice amount of the Chicago skyline. It made me feel sick for some reason. I felt like my city was killing me mentally. Every time I thought about the things I had been through inside of it, all I could feel was heartache and pain. There had been so many losses.

I shook my head to knock me out of that depressing zone. "Yo, both of y'all get y'all assess down there and suck on me. I'm talking I wanna see you kiss over my shit."

Tonya joined Lacey on her knees. They took turns kissing all over my dick, and each other. Tonya stroked me, looking into my eyes. "I'd do anything for you, TJ. I mean that shit." She grabbed my piece from Lacey and went to work on it. Sucking loudly.

I shivered. Lacey stood up and stripped down to her red see-through lingerie panties and bra. My hand went between them thick thighs almost immediately, and into her underwear. She groaned and spaced her thighs.

Tonya stood up. "Come on, let's move this to the bed." She undressed; only left on her garter belt and stockings. Then she laid back on the bed and spread her legs wide. Her pussy was on full display.

Lacey laid on top of her with her back to her chest. Now I had two pussies right on top of one another staring back at me. I climbed between them and eased into Tonya first. She moaned, and shivered as hard as I did when she'd first sucked me into her mouth. "Baby. You so thick."

I laid on top of Lacey and got to pounding Tonya out. Lacey sat up, and bit into my neck. "Fuck her, Daddy. Fuck her lil' pussy for me, too."

I sped up the pace. Her sex lips sucked at me hungrily. She kept moaning louder and louder with every inch that she got until my hips were banging into her pelvis. A slushing sound resonated from between our thighs.

"Unn. Unn. Unn. Daddy. Unn. Shit. Harder, Daddy. Harder." She dug her nails into Lacey's thick thighs.

Lacey shook, and slid her tongue into my mouth. My hand went under her bra. Tweaked her hard nipples, pulling on them. She yelped and sucked more passionately on my tongue. "Me next, Daddy. Me next." She took my piece out of Tonya and slid it into her. She bucked, rolled off of her, giving me her ass from the back while she planted her face into the bed. Her ass spread open revealing both holes. The bottom one leaking. The top slightly pink, and crinkled.

I grabbed her hair and waited for Tonya to slide me into her. As soon as she did, I went crazy, fucking like my life depended on it. "Uhhhh! Uhhhh! Yes! Yes! Tonya, he. Uhhhh!" She started to bounce back into me over and over again. The bed rocked on its frame. The headboard tapped at the wall.

Tonya laid beside us and fingered herself while she watched her friend get pounded out. She was going at herself so good that I forgot all about what I was doing to Lacey until she screamed that she was cumming. She ripped at the sheets and came, shaking like crazy.

I pulled out of her and went back into Tonya. Tonya laid on her back and wrapped her ankles around my waist while I gave her the business. She opened her mouth wide and breathed heavily. I could feel her walls working on me. Her pussy got wetter and wetter. She arched her back and took everything I was giving her like a champion. When she came, she sat all the way up, and pulled me down on top other while my hips kept pounding away.

I rolled off of her, and Lacey slid down on me. She bit into my neck. Then she was riding me fast with her titties bouncing up and down on her chest. She held my shoulders. Sweat sliding down the side of her face. "Ooo. Ooo. Ooo. Yes!" Faster and faster. "Daddy!

Daddy. Ooo. Shit. That grown dick!" She closed her eyes, and fell on me, twerking her pussy.

I came, squeezing her ass. Shooting jet after jet into her tight womb. She must've felt them because the next thing I knew she was bucking under me, and shaking like crazy.

Tonya pulled her off of me, and pushed her knees to her chest. She lowered her face, and got to slurping up the both of our messes with her ass in the air. Her fat cat leaked. It was golden brown, and oozing. Lacey moaned. Shaking every few seconds with her eyes closed.

My phone vibrated on the dresser. I sat up and kissed Tonya on her ass. Sliding my tongue into her backdoor before I scooted out of the bed. I walked over to the dresser and grabbed my phone. My piece shiny with both girls' juices all over it.

There was a message from Juelz. It read: *Found Deion. What you wanna do?*

I stared at the message for a long time. I felt like I couldn't breathe. Deion was the last piece of the puzzle that I needed to figure out before I could move on with my life. I had to have him. I texted: *Where U at?*

There was a slight delay. His response: *When I get back to da Land I'ma hit you up.*

Tonya came behind me, and slid her hand around taking a hold or my swipe. "Let me clean that off for you, Daddy." She dropped to her knees, and did just that.

Lacey curled up on her side, and sucked on her thumb. Her thick thighs did a poor job of covering up her cat. I could see her folds as clear as day. It made me want to jump back up in that pussy again.

***

After we showered, I hugged up with both girls, waiting impatiently for Juelz to hit me up. I had so many questions. I was wondering how it was that he'd stumbled across Deion. Did he say anything to him? What kind of security did he have around him? I prayed that I could catch him slipping, and finish him off. It seemed like I had been chasing him forever.

Tonya kissed my chest, and nestled up against me. "TJ, do you think I'm weird if I tell you that I love you?"

Lacey's eyes popped open. "Girl, you not supposed to say shit like that to a boss. We always learned that when you start to expressing your feelings and what not, that's when a boss a kick your ass to the curb and replace you. So, girl, shut up." Lacey rolled her eyes.

"You shut up. I wanna tell him how I feel. I don't care what you're talking about. TJ, can you please answer my question?"

"What's your question, baby?"

She sighed. "I said. If I told you that I love you, would you think that I'm weird?"

"N'all, baby, but you don't love me." I said, pulling her close to me.

"Yes, I do. How you gon' tell me that I don't?" She seemed offended.

"Well, let's go this route. Why do you love me, Tonya?"

She sat up, with her breasts jiggling on her chest. "Because, before you came into the picture, me and Lacey were starving, and struggling to make it. So were our families. But now you make sure that we're good. Why wouldn't I love you?"

"Baby, you appreciate me. You don't love me."

"Yes, I do."

"Let me ask you a question. If I died tomorrow would you cry?"

"Yeah, don't say that. Of course, I would cry." Tonya whined.

"I would too. I don't even wanna think about no shit like that happening. I know it would be normal because people are dying every day, but still, that would crush me." Lacey added.

I smiled. "Y'all are alright with me. Yo, I love you too, Tonya."

"You fa real, or are you just saying that?"

"I'm fa real. I got mad love for you and Lacey." I kissed both girls on the lips.

Tonya licked hers. "Okay, tell me something. What makes you love me?"

I laughed. She was so adorable. I could tell that she starved for my affection. "I love you because you always quick to pop that cannon for me. And I love you because you so ma'fuckin' fine. You're my baby. Killas love too, Shorty." I hugged her closer to me. "That enough for you?"

190

She smiled and closed her eyes. "Hell yeah, ain't no man ever told me he loved me. Not even my father. Thank you, TJ. I love you more." She started to doze off beside me.

Lacey stared at me with her big hazel eyes. "Do you love me too? I mean, I do love you too. You know, like she does and all that."

I nodded. "Yeah, Lacey. I love you too. Now let's pass out until Juelz get up with me."

"Wait a minute, TJ. Do you honestly think that something is about to happen to you fa real?" Tonya opened her eyes so she could hear what I had to say. She looked worried, and afraid.

"Yo, we live in Chicago. Shit happens all the time. I don't know what my day to day look like." I closed my eyes. "But it's good to know that y'all care."

Tonya hopped out of the bed naked and slammed her fist into her little hand. "I swear to God, Daddy, if anything happen to you, I'ma turn this city upside down. Them niggas out there don't think a female can get down like that, but they'll be sadly mistaken. I'm riding for you, Daddy, until my last breath."

Lacey blinked tears. "Yo, it's whatever, Shorty. Fa real. My loyalty is to you, TJ."

I held my arms out, and both of them climbed back in the bed. They got under each arm, and snuggled back to me. "Yo, it's good to know that I got two ride a die bitches beside me. That make me wanna smoke a ma'fucka fa y'all. Word up."

Tonya looked up at me. "Just stay alive, Daddy. That's all we ask."

"Yeah, that's it. Chicago is cold enough. We need your security, and warmth." Lacey added.

"I got y'all." We all hugged up and dozed off to sleep.

Chapter 20

"You gotta excuse me for being late, TJ. I had another more serious matter that I had to tend to." Juelz said when he pulled up on me, rolling a black Jaguar four nights later. The windows were tinted pitch black. He had a black bandana around his neck. I could tell that he was ready to ride on a nigga.

I got into the Jaguar, and slammed the door. "It's all good. What's the business though?"

"That fool Jay tripping. I had to turn down a move out there in Phoenix that he wanted me to handle. Now he got his panties all in a bunch and shit. You know how that shit go when a mafucka so used to you saying yes that when you finally say no they get to acting all funny and shit." He pulled off.

"Yeah. But fuck dude; what's up with Deion? Where he supposed to be at?" I asked, cutting straight to the chase.

"That nigga fuckin' around over there in Moetown. He got a few highest that's honoring him like he a Prince a something."

"Word?"

Juelz nodded. "I hear he fuckin' with that heroin now too. Tough."

"It was only a matter of time. He grew up with my pops being his role model. You should've already known where that was going to get him?"

"Yeah, well, hopefully we be able to handle that nigga then we won't have to worry about his ass no more. I feel like we been chasing behind what happened to Marie for a million years."

I nodded. "Well, let's go end this shit. I'm ready to get on with my life too."

"It ain't that simple though. You see, Deion is a major nigga in the game now. He moving a lot of weight, and since he is, he's been real useful to the Cartel. You already know how they get down."

"Nigga, so what is you saying?" I was getting irritated.

"I'm saying that if we hit this nigga, we finna have some serious consequences to deal with because it will be an unsanctioned hit. The Cartel frowns upon that, especially if it messes with their money flow."

"Yo, so you saying that this nigga get a pass for what he did to my little sister? Are you fucking kidding me?" I snapped, ready to punch Juelz in his jaw.

Juelz shook his head. "Nigga, chill. I ain't saying that. You already know ain't no hoe in me. I'm asking you if you think it'll be worth it to war over? And I ain't just talking about no regular war either. I'm talking some all-out serious heat from them ma'fuckin' killas down south. You think that's worth it?"

"You muthafuckin' right." I didn't give a fuck who I had to go up against. Deion had to pay for what he'd done to Marie. There was no way around that. If that meant that a mafucka was gon' kill me right after I killed him then so be it. That vengeance shit ran cold in my blood.

"Aiight then. We gotta do what we gotta do then." He got to texting on his phone after he pulled up to a stop sign. It took him a few minutes to write it, then he pulled back off. "Shorty, you already know that I'm rolling with you until the wheels fall off."

"I know that. Let's handle this last bit of business and be done wit' it."

Juelz's phone buzzed again. He read the message and frowned. "Dawg, I gotta go holler at Jay real quick."

"Man, fuck Jay. We gotta knock off Deion."

Juelz shook his head. "This shit serious, nigga. I gotta go holler at dude whether I want to or not." He looked sick.

"Fuck you mean?"

"It's just one of those things, TJ. Let me handle this right quick and we'll go twist that nigga cap back in a minute. That's my word."

"Yeah, nigga, whatever. Let's just go."

***

Jay was a big ass white boy that stood five-feet-ten inches tall. He was bald with a reddish, gray beard. His eyes were hazel. They looked menacing. He had tattoos all over his neck and arms. He was Juelz's direct plug from Chicago to the Cartels south of the border. It was because of him that Juelz had been able to come up so quick in the game.

Juelz pulled into the garage of Jay's auto repair shop. Jay stood in the middle of the floor almost daring Juelz to hit him as he pulled in. I was so irritated that had I been driving I may have. After Juelz pulled into the garage, the door was lowered. Jay's men seemed to come out of the shadows with assault rifles in their hands. They aimed them at the car.

"Juelz, what the fuck is this?" I snapped, looking over to him.

"Nigga, be smooth. This nigga just acting like a bitch right now. Whatever you do, don't help me. It's just a process. Trust me." He lowered the window and stuck his hands out of it. "Yo, Jay, call off your dogs."

Jay walked over to the car with a mug on his face. He yanked opened the door and pulled Juelz out of it. "You no good muthafucker. You think you can say no to me after I made your ass?" He threw him to the ground and kicked him in the stomach.

I placed my hand on the handle of my gun. I was ready to go for what I knew. Fuck Juelz's orders for me to not help him. How could I not when this big ass white dude was treating him like he was?

He yanked Juelz up, and slammed him to the wall. Upped a Glock .9, and stuffed it in his mouth. "You wanna tell me no now, boy? Huh?"

Juelz closed his eyes. I could see his chest heaving. His hands balled into fists off and on. A thick vein appeared in his neck.

"Aw, you're tough, right? You got a few murders under your belt, and you think you're tough now? Huh? You project filth! You don't ever say no to me. You're done." He spat in his face, and threw him to the ground again, cocked his pistol and aimed it down at Juelz. He took one step back and got to firing his gun over and over again.

"Noooooo!" I heard myself hollering as I ran toward them with both guns in my hands.

Before I could make it to them, the garage door raised, and I saw a bunch of flashlights, and police suited in SWAT gear with assault rifles in their hands.

"Freeze! Freeze! Freeze! Police! Get on the ground! Now!"

To Be Continued…
Born Heartless 4
Coming Soon

Submission Guideline

Submit the first three chapters of your completed manuscript to ldpsubmissions@gmail.com, subject line: Your book's title. The manuscript must be in a .doc file and sent as an attachment. Document should be in Times New Roman, double spaced and in size 12 font. Also, provide your synopsis and full contact information. If sending multiple submissions, they must each be in a separate email.

Have a story but no way to send it electronically? You can still submit to LDP/Ca$h Presents. Send in the first three chapters, written or typed, of your completed manuscript to:

LDP: Submissions Dept
Po Box 870494
Mesquite, Tx 75187

DO NOT send original manuscript. Must be a duplicate.

Provide your synopsis and a cover letter containing your full contact information.

Thanks for considering LDP and Ca$h Presents.

<u>Coming Soon from Lock Down Publications/Ca$h Presents</u>

BOW DOWN TO MY GANGSTA

By **Ca$h**

TORN BETWEEN TWO

By **Coffee**

STEADY MOBBIN **III**

By **Marcellus Allen**

BLOOD OF A BOSS **VI**

SHADOWS OF THE GAME II

By **Askari**

LOYAL TO THE GAME **IV**

By **T.J. & Jelissa**

A DOPEBOY'S PRAYER **II**

By **Eddie "Wolf" Lee**

IF LOVING YOU IS WRONG… **III**

By **Jelissa**

TRUE SAVAGE **VII**

MIDNIGHT CARTEL

DOPE BOY MAGIC II

By **Chris Green**

BLAST FOR ME **III**

DUFFLE BAG CARTEL **IV**

HEARTLESS GOON **IV**

A SAVAGE DOPEBOY II

T.J. Edwards

DRUG LORDS III
By **Ghost**
A HUSTLER'S DECEIT III
KILL ZONE **II**
BAE BELONGS TO ME III
SOUL OF A MONSTER III
By **Aryanna**
THE COST OF LOYALTY **III**
By **Kweli**
THE SAVAGE LIFE III
CHAINED TO THE STREETS II
By **J-Blunt**
KING OF NEW YORK V
COKE KINGS IV
BORN HEARTLESS IV
By **T.J. Edwards**
GORILLAZ IN THE BAY V
De'Kari
THE STREETS ARE CALLING II
Duquie Wilson
KINGPIN KILLAZ IV
STREET KINGS III
PAID IN BLOOD III
CARTEL KILLAZ IV
Hood Rich

200

SINS OF A HUSTLA II

ASAD

TRIGGADALE III

Elijah R. Freeman

KINGZ OF THE GAME V

Playa Ray

SLAUGHTER GANG IV

RUTHLESS HEART II

By Willie Slaughter

THE HEART OF A SAVAGE II

By Jibril Williams

FUK SHYT II

By Blakk Diamond

THE DOPEMAN'S BODYGAURD II

By Tranay Adams

TRAP GOD II

By Troublesome

YAYO II

A SHOOTER'S AMBITION II

By S. Allen

GHOST MOB

Stilloan Robinson

KINGPIN DREAMS II

By Paper Boi Rari

CREAM

T.J. Edwards

By Yolanda Moore
SON OF A DOPE FIEND II
By Renta
FOREVER GANGSTA II
By Adrian Dulan
LOYALTY AIN'T PROMISED
By Keith Williams
THE PRICE YOU PAY FOR LOVE II
By Destiny Skai
THE LIFE OF A HOOD STAR
By Rashia Wilson
TOE TAGZ II
By Ah'Million
CONFESSIONS OF A GANGSTA II
By Nicholas Lock

Available Now

RESTRAINING ORDER **I & II**
By **CA$H & Coffee**
LOVE KNOWS NO BOUNDARIES **I II & III**
By **Coffee**
RAISED AS A GOON I, II, III & IV
BRED BY THE SLUMS I, II, III

Born Heartless 3

BLAST FOR ME I & II
ROTTEN TO THE CORE I II III
A BRONX TALE I, II, III
DUFFEL BAG CARTEL I II III
HEARTLESS GOON
A SAVAGE DOPEBOY
HEARTLESS GOON I II III
DRUG LORDS I II
By **Ghost**
LAY IT DOWN **I & II**
LAST OF A DYING BREED
BLOOD STAINS OF A SHOTTA I & II III
By **Jamaica**
LOYAL TO THE GAME
LOYAL TO THE GAME II
LOYAL TO THE GAME III
LIFE OF SIN I, II III
By **TJ & Jelissa**
BLOODY COMMAS I & II
SKI MASK CARTEL I II & III
KING OF NEW YORK I II,III IV
RISE TO POWER I II III
COKE KINGS I II III
BORN HEARTLESS I II III
By **T.J. Edwards**

T.J. Edwards

IF LOVING HIM IS WRONG…I & II
LOVE ME EVEN WHEN IT HURTS I II III
By **Jelissa**
WHEN THE STREETS CLAP BACK I & II III
By **Jibril Williams**
A DISTINGUISHED THUG STOLE MY HEART I II & III
LOVE SHOULDN'T HURT I II III IV
RENEGADE BOYS I II III IV
By **Meesha**
A GANGSTER'S CODE I &, II III
A GANGSTER'S SYN I II III
THE SAVAGE LIFE I II
CHAINED TO THE STREETS
By J-Blunt
PUSH IT TO THE LIMIT
By **Bre' Hayes**
BLOOD OF A BOSS **I, II, III, IV, V**
SHADOWS OF THE GAME
By **Askari**
THE STREETS BLEED MURDER **I, II & III**
THE HEART OF A GANGSTA I II& III
By **Jerry Jackson**
CUM FOR ME
CUM FOR ME 2
CUM FOR ME 3

Born Heartless 3

CUM FOR ME 4

CUM FOR ME 5

An **LDP Erotica Collaboration**

BRIDE OF A HUSTLA **I II & II**

THE FETTI GIRLS **I, II& III**

CORRUPTED BY A GANGSTA I, II III, IV

BLINDED BY HIS LOVE

THE PRICE YOU PAY FOR LOVE

By **Destiny Skai**

WHEN A GOOD GIRL GOES BAD

By **Adrienne**

THE COST OF LOYALTY I II

By Kweli

A GANGSTER'S REVENGE **I II III & IV**

THE BOSS MAN'S DAUGHTERS

THE BOSS MAN'S DAUGHTERS II

THE BOSSMAN'S DAUGHTERS III

THE BOSSMAN'S DAUGHTERS IV

THE BOSS MAN'S DAUGHTERS **V**

A SAVAGE LOVE **I & II**

BAE BELONGS TO ME I II

A HUSTLER'S DECEIT I, II, III

WHAT BAD BITCHES DO I, II, III

SOUL OF A MONSTER I II

KILL ZONE

T.J. Edwards

By **Aryanna**
A KINGPIN'S AMBITON
A KINGPIN'S AMBITION **II**
I MURDER FOR THE DOUGH
By **Ambitious**
TRUE SAVAGE
TRUE SAVAGE II
TRUE SAVAGE **III**
TRUE SAVAGE **IV**
TRUE SAVAGE **V**
TRUE SAVAGE **VI**
DOPE BOY MAGIC
MIDNIGHT CARTEL
By **Chris Green**
A DOPEBOY'S PRAYER
By **Eddie "Wolf" Lee**
THE KING CARTEL **I, II & III**
By **Frank Gresham**
THESE NIGGAS AIN'T LOYAL **I, II & III**
By **Nikki Tee**
GANGSTA SHYT **I II &III**
By **CATO**
THE ULTIMATE BETRAYAL
By **Phoenix**
BOSS'N UP **I , II & III**

206

Born Heartless 3

By **Royal Nicole**
I LOVE YOU TO DEATH
By Destiny J
I RIDE FOR MY HITTA
I STILL RIDE FOR MY HITTA
By **Misty Holt**
LOVE & CHASIN' PAPER
By **Qay Crockett**
TO DIE IN VAIN
SINS OF A HUSTLA
By **ASAD**
BROOKLYN HUSTLAZ
By **Boogsy Morina**
BROOKLYN ON LOCK I & II
By **Sonovia**
GANGSTA CITY
By **Teddy Duke**
A DRUG KING AND HIS DIAMOND I & II III
A DOPEMAN'S RICHES
HER MAN, MINE'S TOO I, II
CASH MONEY HO'S
By Nicole Goosby
TRAPHOUSE KING **I II & III**
KINGPIN KILLAZ I II III
STREET KINGS I II

T.J. Edwards

PAID IN BLOOD **I II**
CARTEL KILLAZ I II III
By **Hood Rich**
LIPSTICK KILLAH **I, II, III**
CRIME OF PASSION I II & III
By **Mimi**
STEADY MOBBN' **I, II, III**
By **Marcellus Allen**
WHO SHOT YA **I, II, III**
SON OF A DOPE FIEND
Renta
GORILLAZ IN THE BAY **I II III IV**
DE'KARI
TRIGGADALE I II
Elijah R. Freeman
GOD BLESS THE TRAPPERS I, II, III
THESE SCANDALOUS STREETS I, II, III
FEAR MY GANGSTA I, II, III
THESE STREETS DON'T LOVE NOBODY I, II
BURY ME A G I, II, III, IV, V
A GANGSTA'S EMPIRE I, II, III, IV
THE DOPEMAN'S BODYGAURD
Tranay Adams
THE STREETS ARE CALLING
Duquie Wilson

MARRIED TO A BOSS... I II III

By Destiny Skai & Chris Green

KINGZ OF THE GAME I II III IV

Playa Ray

SLAUGHTER GANG I II III

RUTHLESS HEART

By Willie Slaughter

THE HEART OF A SAVAGE

By Jibril Williams

FUK SHYT

By Blakk Diamond

DON'T F#CK WITH MY HEART I II

By Linnea

ADDICTED TO THE DRAMA I II III

By Jamila

YAYO

A SHOOTER'S AMBITION

By S. Allen

TRAP GOD

By Troublesome

FOREVER GANGSTA

By Adrian Dulan

TOE TAGZ

By Ah'Million

KINGPIN DREAMS

T.J. Edwards

By Paper Boi Rari

CONFESSIONS OF A GANGSTA

By Nicholas Lock

BOOKS BY LDP'S CEO, CA$H

TRUST IN NO MAN

TRUST IN NO MAN 2

TRUST IN NO MAN 3

BONDED BY BLOOD

SHORTY GOT A THUG

THUGS CRY

THUGS CRY 2

THUGS CRY 3

TRUST NO BITCH

TRUST NO BITCH 2

TRUST NO BITCH 3

TIL MY CASKET DROPS

RESTRAINING ORDER

RESTRAINING ORDER 2

IN LOVE WITH A CONVICT

Coming Soon

BONDED BY BLOOD 2

BOW DOWN TO MY GANGSTA

T.J. Edwards